The
Fourth Person
Within

By SGT Roy Jones

This book is FICTIONAL
(or maybe NOT)

I sincerely hope and pray this book helps
some of our veterans who do not understand
what has happened to them.

This Book is dedicated

to

Staff Sergeant Jack Jackson

and all of the other heroes who have faced

"The Fourth Person Within."

and special thanks to

Colonel Jim Lee, ret.

for all his help in making this book a reality.

CHAPTERS

THE FOURTH PERSON WITHIN

It is my opinion that within each of us, there are four people:

#1. That person who we project, that person we want people to think we are.

#2 That person who we are perceived to be, who never seems to match what we are trying to project.

#3. That person who we really are, deep inside. That person who we protect and rarely share with anyone. This person is so tender and easily hurt that we are afraid to share him.

#4. 'The Fourth Person Within,' who is rarely seen, and only shows up in extreme circumstances. When we are in life-or-death situations, or when we see or experience something so horrible that our minds cannot process it. 'The Fourth Person Within' can be mean, vicious and unforgiving, making him very difficult to control. He causes us to do things we never would have believed we were capable of doing.

The sights we see and the actions we take, when at war give rise to 'The Fourth Person Within' in many of us. Some may become consumed by him and never leave him behind. Some try to drown him in alcohol, some try to hide from him with drugs, some commit suicide to escape him. As for me, I was blessed enough to see him for what he was and leave him behind. This is my story.

THE BEGINNING

I grew up – or was snatched up – in Memphis, Tennessee.

I have no memory of a father, so I always referred to him as my "sperm donor." My sperm donor was away at World War II and my younger sister, my mother and I lived for a time with my grandfather and the rest of our extended family. I have 12 aunts, one of whom is one year younger, and another who is one year older than I am. My grandfather was, to me, a superhero. He worked 5 miles down the road at the sawmill and walked to work 5 or 6 days a week. He raised crops on-shares with a more fortunate neighbor. My grandparents had that old-fashioned pioneer spirit that built this country. They believed that you worked hard and did anything possible to take care of others without thinking about your own comfort. There were about 15 people living in that old house in the country including a lot of children (mostly girls). There was a pump in the kitchen for water; the bathroom was a little house out back. I think I was about 5 or 6 years old when we got electricity. That meant one light in each room and a radio.

My earliest memory was laying on a pallet on the living room floor. One cold winter morning, I lay there watching my grandfather get up about 4 a.m. to paddle into the kitchen where he started a fire in the cook stove, put on a pot of coffee, and went to the living room to stoke the wood fire we used for heat. My grandmother would get up and go to the kitchen where she and my grandfather would have a cup of coffee. This was to be the only peace they would have all day. They would just sit quietly and sip on their coffee, I remember laying there and watching all of this happen. I thought my grandfather must be the strongest man in the world. He was always the first one up preparing the way for the rest of the family. I vividly remember thinking, one day I want to be as strong as my grandfather. I want to be able to have people depend on me the way we all depended on him. After coffee, grandma would begin making biscuits and gravy for breakfast.

It seemed to me that my grandfather worked every day from before daylight until well after dark. He did, however, take time to teach me to hunt with a single shot 22 rifle, which I still have. He taught me how to shoot, one shot for one dead animal for supper. Rabbits and squirrels mostly with the occasional raccoon. When I was seven or eight years old, Grandpa would give me three bullets and send me out to bring back supper. To him, that meant three animals for the cook pot, so if I shot and missed, I was in trouble. That meant I had to try to run down a rabbit with a stick, and that never happened. Fortunately for me, my grandfather also taught me how to set snares and traps. We would go fishing two or three times a year. My grandfather would take 2 or 3 lbs. of cornmeal and put it in a "tote sack," and hang it in the water from a limb. He would do this on a Wednesday knowing we would be back on Saturday. The cornmeal would slowly leak out of the bag, which attracted small fish, which attracted the larger fish. We would borrow a net from our neighbor down the road that had floats on top of it and weights on the bottom. The net was about 50 ft long; we would straighten it out along the bank then anchor one end and swing the other end out into the river in a large circle bringing it back to where it was anchored. Usually the net was full of fish of all sizes, a few turtles, and the occasional snake or two. At this point the real work began. We cleaned the fish and turtles to harvest the meat. Then, we always gave a generous portion of our bounty to the family that had loaned us the net.

The fall was always busy. After harvesting the crops, it was time to kill hogs to furnish meat for the year. Again, the neighbors were all involved. Killing hogs, cutting them up, and salting the meat is a big job. The only part of the hog that we did not eat was the squeal. I will not go into the details of how it is done so you can keep enjoying your breakfast.

On rare occasions in the fall, a lot of the men in the area got together to go coon hunting. Everyone had coon dogs. One time they let me go and carry the gun. Coon hunting is always done at night and some alcohol may be involved. We sat on top of a high hill and listened to the dogs bark. As they ran the coon, at some point the tone of their bark would change - meaning they had treed a coon. We took off down the hill and headed for the sound. The dogs were happily jumping up and down at the base of a large tree when we finally arrived. A couple of the men built a fire, and everyone was trying to spot the coon. My Uncle Johnny was elected to climb the tree to knock the coon out of the tree. Uncle Johnny had a tough job because, if the dogs had treed a bobcat instead of a coon, he would not know it until it was too late, and he could be in a heck of a mess. The gun I carried was a 12-gauge shotgun. I was lying on the ground with the shotgun propped up against a stump pretending to aim at where I thought the coon was. The gun went off and Uncle Johnny fell out of the tree. I thought I had shot him and took off at a dead run into the night. In the confusion, I got away. I was scared I had shot my Uncle Johnny.

As it turned out, he did not get hit, but either way I was in a lot of trouble. I ran a long way and hid in the woods. I stayed away until hunger drove me back home the next night. Like a thief, I came sneaking up to the back door. I heard everyone talking and laughing about Johnny falling out of the tree. As I walked into the room, it got eerily quiet and everyone just stared at me. I must have looked a real mess, "Come on in" my grandfather said. Johnny was sitting there all scratched up, but he wasn't as mad as I thought he would be. My grandfather said, "What did you learn last night? What you should have learned is that guns are not toys and when you put your finger on the trigger you intend to kill something. Always remember that." "I have," I said. A lot of the lessons I have learned in my life were learned the hard way – this being one of those.

My grandfather taught me to hunt and fish for food, not for fun. "Never kill anything you are not going to eat" he would say. He also taught me self-reliance, honesty, and a strong work ethic. Since I have no good memories of my sperm donor (father), my grandfather and Uncle Johnny were the only male role models in my life. To be totally honest, my sister who is 4 years younger than me, calls him her father. My grandfather and Uncle Johnny were the only males of which I have any good memories of, and I seem to be their entertainment center. From them, I learned about snipe hunting and the like.

ORPHANAGE

When I was about 9 years old, my mother moved my sister and me to Memphis, the big city. It was not long before my sister and I found ourselves in St Peter's orphanage for safekeeping. Mom worked 3 jobs and came to spend every Sunday afternoon with us. We were housed at St. Peter's orphanage for about a year and half, while Mom worked and saved so that we could get our lives together.

At St Peter's Orphanage I experienced a lot of trauma. I was nine years old and cross-eyed, and all the kids liked to pick on me. I tried to play baseball with them, but every small mistake I made was amplified due to my affliction. I had never played baseball before. Having no friends, I spent all my time alone. While sitting alone one day I was thinking is this how my life is to be, being pushed around all the time with everyone making fun of me?

What would my grandfather do? I could not see him sitting around and being picked on, so I decided to fight back as best I could. It certainly could not be any worse. The next time one of the larger boys pushed me down and everyone laughed, I got up and hit him hard in the mouth. My fist hurt, but it hurt him a whole lot worse. Everyone was in shock. This was a turning point in my life. From that day on, if you pushed me, watch out. I push back hard. Over the next few days I had several altercations. People began saying, "Watch out for the cross-eyed guy. He's crazy." I still did not have any friends, but everyone left me alone. One of the nuns took me to the gym. "You like to fight?" she asked, "Well, we are going to fight." She handed me a pair of boxing gloves; I did not know what to do. "Put them on" she said, so I did. "I can't fight you," I said. I was raised never to hit a female under any circumstances. There we stood - a nun built like a refrigerator and a skinny kid from the country prepared for mortal combat. "If you won't fight, you'd better defend yourself she said and started swinging. As protection, I held my hands up in front of my face. But she beat me bloody anyway. She took me to the dispensary and left actually thinking she had accomplished something. She did, but not what she thought – she just gave me more reason to get even.

I was mostly healed by Sunday afternoon when Mom came to visit. She looked at me and said, "What happened to you?" "No big deal." I said, "Wrestling around with some of the guys" and left it at that.

There was a large dining hall with a six-foot open space between the two sides-girls on one side and boys on the other side. You sat in the same chair for every meal. Mealtime was the only time you ever saw the girls. There was a cute girl that sat about four rows up from me and since we both sat on the aisle, I could see her really well. I thought she was really something. She did not know that I was alive. One day I nudged the boy next to me and said, "You see that brown-haired girl up there" and pointed to her, "That is my girlfriend." The boy told a nun I had a girlfriend and I was taken to the office and accused of being a sex maniac. Once again, I was severely beaten.

Early one Monday morning they took me to St Joseph's Hospital. I had no idea why. They examined my right eye and that afternoon they operated on it. When I came to after the operation, I was in a ward with both eyes bandaged and could not see anything. They had not explained anything to me. I stayed in that ward all alone for a week with no one speaking to me except the occasional nurse. My mother did not come and see me, no one did. Here I am ten years old, in a strange place, just sitting all alone. In my mind, I had been abandoned by everyone on this earth and felt no one cared for me or loved me anymore. I have never felt so alone in my life and I went into deep depression. It seemed like an eternity. Five days later, the doctor came in, took the bandages off my eyes, and examined them. After prescribing glasses for me, I didn't see him anymore. Saturday morning, they gave me the glasses and took me back to St Peter's orphanage. Now the kids would call me four eyes instead of cross eyes, but they never did it within reach.

BACK TOGETHER

Sunday afternoon mom showed up, "Where did you get those glasses?" she asked. "At the hospital" I said. "Hospital. What hospital?" "The one where they operated on my eye" I replied. Mom went into a rage. That was the moment when I realized she had no idea I had been taken to the hospital. My mother was a tall beautiful redheaded lady and I watched as that red hair turned into flames before my very eyes. I don't know what she said to those people in the office, but it was not good. Within 3 weeks Mom had taken us out of St Peters. Mom had been working hard and saving every penny she could. Finally, she got enough to put a small down payment on a 3-room house at 880 Blythe Street in Memphis.

The front door opened into the living room; then the bedroom, the kitchen, and bathroom. It was called a shotgun house. That was the entire house, but it was perfect for us. Mom quit one of her jobs and kept two of them. She would work at Harmon's Bakery from eight am until three pm- five days a week. She was a server at Fracas' Pit BBQ in the evening five or six nights a week. Mom hired a lady as a housekeeper and babysitter so we would not be alone at night.

There was no such thing as social assistance in those days so if you did not work, you did not eat. I can only imagine what my mother must have gone through physically and emotionally in those days. I had to grow up fast. I learned to cook, to sew, to iron clothes, and to look after my baby sister. I tried to help every way I could. I was trying to be the man of the house at age 11. Once a month mom would give me three streetcar tokens and send me to downtown Memphis to pay the Light Gas and Water Bill. She gave me three tokens because I had to transfer one time to get there, and if I made a mistake and got on the wrong streetcar, I still had an extra token to get back home. That was a lot of responsibility for an 11 or 12-year-old boy, but mom had faith in me and that meant an awful lot. Sis and I walked to school every day when mom was at work. There's only so much you can do with that many free hours.

Some Saturdays, during the warm weather, I would ride my bike to a neighborhood called Chickasaw Gardens. There was a nice lake there, and I would spend the entire day by myself just fishing and exploring. Late in the afternoon, I would ride home with my catch. I always had four to six small-to-medium size catfish. When I got home, I knew I had to clean those fish so that we could have them Sunday. Mom did not seem to worry about me too much. She knew how self-reliant I was and that I could take care of myself. We lived in that house for three or four years while Mom slowly fixed it up. She sold it for enough money that we could move into a larger fixer-upper house. That was her plan; buy a fixer-upper live in it for several years, then sell it to make enough money to move into a larger fixer upper.

Mom remarried and we moved to the suburbs. Sis and I rode the school bus to school. I was in the 9th grade and played on Germantown's first football team. There were only 21 players on the team, and we were not very large. I was in the 9th grade playing tackle on a senior high football team at about a hundred and sixty pounds. I normally would be facing a player that weighed 250 to 270 pounds. We lost every game we played that year, but we did not always lose the fight. That is where I learned, "it is not the size of the dog in the fight but the size of fight in the dog" that really matters.

I fought in the Golden Gloves that year and had three fights. The first fight I knocked my opponent out of the ring in the first round; the second fight I knocked my opponent out in the second round.

I was starting to get cocky, so the third fight they actually put me in the ring with a real boxer, who wore me out. He hit me so many times it was embarrassing – he could not hit me hard enough to really hurt me – but he made me very angry. When I came out of the corner for the third round, I was carrying that three-legged stool you sit on in the corner. I was going to mess him up. They threw me out of the gym and barred me from ever fighting in the Golden Gloves again. I now know I am not a boxer; but a street fighter.

That year at Germantown I played football, basketball, and ran track. I was the second-string center on the basketball team. I still have the big red "G" that I earned for playing sports that year.

I was also introduced to "The Red Badge of Courage." which was a paddle the principal kept in his office. He bent me over so far that my head was about 3 inches from the door jamb, and he told me to hold my hands behind my back. He said, "He was going to work on this end and the other end was my problem. When he hit me with that paddle my head went into the door jam. After 5 licks I was staggering. He almost knocked me out. My 9th grade math teacher did not like me because when she put a math problem on the board, and I could give her the right answer, but I couldn't tell her how I got it. She expected me to explain all of my calculations and I just couldn't do it; I just knew the answer. She told the principal that it would be a waste of time for the school and me to take any further math, so I happily never did.

Mom's marriage did not last, so we moved back into the city. I began the 10th grade at Treadwell High School the largest school I had ever seen. I found a job to have spending money, working on the weekends in the movie theater for fifty cents an hour. Later, I took a job at National Food Stores grocery store, then on to Rooks Exxon. I was staying busy and really enjoying the spending money.

I met Sandy Clark, the love of my life, I thought. We had what you might call an on-and-off relationship. I think her mother liked me more than Sandy. On one occasion, Sandy told me she had a date Friday night with a football player from Ole Miss. If she was trying to make me jealous, it really worked. When the guy arrived at her house, I was hiding in the bushes. As he stopped the car, I ran over and told him to leave. I don't remember what he said but it was probably not very nice. He opened the car door and put his foot on the ground. I slammed the car door on his leg. His leg was broken, he was screaming, and it did not seem to me that's where I needed to be, so I left hurriedly. What Sandy had not told me was that this guy was her cousin and he was coming to dinner with the family that night.

Now I have the entire Ole Miss Football team wanting to kill me for crippling one of their star players and Sandy and her family were not happy with me at all. It took a long while for Sandy and me to get back together again, but I was persistent if nothing else. I just looked at some of our prom pictures and Sandy is still one of the most beautiful women I have ever seen in my life. Prom night I had promised Sandy's mom that I would have her home by 2 a.m.

Well, that did not happen. I got into a fight and when I hit the guy in the nose blood splattered everywhere including all over Sandy. She was trying to stop me, and her dress got torn. Now there's no way I can take her home looking like this, so we went to my house. Now I want you to picture this, your son wakes you up at 2 in the morning. When you open your eyes, you see him standing there with his girlfriend, her dress is torn and they both have blood all over them. Your son is saying "Mom, we are in trouble!"

My poor mother, it is a wonder she did not have a heart attack. I explained, as best I could, what happened. Mom got up and helped Sandy get cleaned up, as best she could. We sat down to talk about it and Mom said, "Son, you created this mess you need to get yourself out of it. I'm going back to bed." Sandy and I stayed at my house a couple of more hours. We decided we were already in so much trouble it could not get any worse, so we decided to go to Shelby Forest where the other kids were going to be that morning.

We did not get 2 miles from my house before Sandy's mother ran us off the road and took her daughter back. She would deal with me later.

I thought to myself, that I had the greatest mother in the world.

NATIONAL GUARD

In April 1956, I was 15 years old and convinced my mother to lie for me and sign an affidavit stating that I was born in 1938. That would make me 17 years old. I joined the National Guard at the ripe old age of 15 and became the lowest form of human life-- a private E-1, in the armed services.

The month of June, we were going to our annual two weeks of training at Fort Gordon, Georgia. We were to travel in convoy. I was now part of the 30th Armored Division and was assigned to the Communications Department of that battalion.

On the morning we were to leave, we were all standing around in the motor pool when a Captain said he needed an assistant driver for that two-and-a-half-ton truck. Everyone froze. "Never Volunteer." Since the captain had no takers, he looked straight at me and said, "Thank you for volunteering, Private Jones." "But sir, I do not have a military driver's license." "Not a problem," he said, and went to his office. When he returned, I had a military driver's license with my name on it. I could not ever let it be known that I was not old enough to have a civilian driver's license.

SO IT BEGAN. I crawled up into the passenger side of that big old truck and tried to look as if I belonged there We pulled out into traffic and I watched that driver like a hawk for the next two hours. After two hours we pulled over to the side to change drivers. Now it was time for me to face my "Moment of Truth." I climbed up into the driver's seat and began to touch everything, scared to death. The regular driver said, "You have never driven a truck before, have you?" "No," I answered. "I have never driven anything this large in my life." Notice I did not say I had never

19

driven any vehicle in my life. He laughed and said, "No problem, I will talk you through as we go." This was one of the many times in my life that God held his protective angel over me. Somehow, we made it to Fort Gordon, Georgia without running off the road or hitting anyone else and I actually became a pretty decent driver that day - thanks to the patience and understanding of the regular driver.

Upon our arrival at Fort Gordon, we set up our area where we would live for the next two weeks. Being the lowest form of human life- a private E-1, I was assigned guard duty the first night. Guard Duty consisted of patrolling around our area driving a Jeep. Of course, having never driven a Jeep, I fell back on my experience driving the truck. About 2 in the morning I was getting pretty cocky about my driving ability, since I had pushed or pulled every knob in that Jeep to figure out what it did. After having driven all day and ending up driving at night, you can get bored and sleepy. So, to stay awake, I started chasing rabbits with the Jeep. That was not the most intelligent thing I have ever done but it kept me awake, until I leaned out of the Jeep to swing at a rabbit, and the Jeep hit a bump and I fell out and then the Jeep came to rest against a large pine tree. What a way to begin my military career!

The communications section ran land lines between all the big guns and the Fire Direction Center (FDC). We had to make sure the wire was well off the road or one of those large vehicles would catch it up in their wheels, thus disrupting Commo. I would run off the road into the tall grass with the wire. On one occasion, I heard a strange rattling noise in front of me. I froze. Then I heard the same noise off to my left and to my right. I had just run into a host of rattlesnakes. I backed away very slowly, very carefully. Then the rattling stopped. My heart began to beat again. From then on, I did not take the wire as far off the road. If the trucks destroyed it, so be it. That was my first, but not the last experience with rattlesnakes.

I spent the next two weeks acting all grown up and like I

belonged there. I drank my first beer that summer. It was over a hundred degrees and the heat had taken out most of the guys working on the big guns, so they made us reposition the gun locations. I cannot remember ever being so hot. On our way back to camp that day someone came up with a case of warm beer. I drank one so fast that I could have won a contest. But it was wet and tasted better than anything I could have imagined. I had a lot of firsts in my life that summer and was really glad when it was all over. We got back to Memphis and to my other life of just being a 15-year-old kid. That is when I realized that I would have to lead two lives. I never talked about being in the National Guard when I was at school and I never talked about being in school when I was with the National Guard. It was almost like being two completely different people, acting one way with one group and another way with the other group.

My work ethic served me well in the National Guard. I began to rise in rank. Evidently, I was demonstrating some leadership skills because over the next three years, I rose to the rank of "Buck" Sergeant (E-5).

U.S. ARMY

I made it through high school and graduated at which time I signed up to join the United States Army. Two weeks after graduation I got on a bus with 43 strangers and went to Fort Leonard Wood, Missouri for basic training. I'd kept my rank as Buck Sergeant, but I had never been to basic training. Thus, began a journey that lasted five long years. I do not know why, but when I left Memphis, I said goodbye to all my friends as if I was never going to return. Somehow, I didn't want anyone to be worrying about me.

The eight weeks of basic training was very tumultuous for me. I had the rank of E-5 Sergeant (SGT) but the knowledge of a buck private, Thank God I was a fast learner.

Our platoon sergeant did not like me because he could tell I was lost. His stripes were all earned in the "real" army. One afternoon he told me to do something that I didn't want to do so I told him; "No, I don't feel like it." He went nuts and asked if we needed to go off somewhere alone and discuss the situation. I said, "You betcha, let's go."

A couple of hours later, he and I left everyone else and went off to settle our differences. He won. He beat me badly. I was admitted to the hospital with cracked ribs and needing stitches in my mouth. They tried to get me to tell them about the fight, but I just said, "What fight? I fell down a flight of stairs face-first."

About three a.m., I got out of bed, put my clothes on, and left the hospital in a lot of pain. I walked across the post to where my barracks was and when my platoon fell out, there I stood. Everyone was shocked. I took my place in the platoon and the Sergeant got in my face and asked me, "How do you feel this morning, Jones?" "Like you got lucky yesterday sergeant," I replied, "Are we going to have to do this thing again?" he asked. "You bet your bottom dollar," I answered.

Now I have never been known to be exceptionally bright and I had been whipped before but never whipped on the second trip. We left and went off by ourselves with the same results. This time when I went to the hospital I was in much worse shape and they tried to get me to tell them that the sergeant had beaten me up so they could press charges against him. I refused; I just said I had a real problem with stairs. They took all my clothes and made me promise not to leave the hospital. About 3 a.m., here I go again this time in an open-back hospital gown, no shoes, and a tremendous amount of pain.

I went from bush to bush and building-to-building across the post until I arrived back at my barracks. I got there just as they fell out. There I stood all bandaged up in an open back hospital gown. No one could believe it. The sergeant did not get in my face this time when he asked me, "How do you feel this morning, Jones?" "Any damn way you want me to, Sergeant. Just please do not ask me to smile. I don't want to break the stitches loose again." They took me back to the hospital where I had to stay for two more days under the watchful eye of the orderlies. I still don't like hospitals.

About a week after I rejoined my platoon, the sergeant asked me to come to his room one evening. I went in sat down and he said, "Jones, I have to tell you something. You scared the hell out of me when you said you thought I got lucky that first morning. I have never seen anyone leave a hospital to go back for more. I don't know if you have more guts than anyone I ever met, or are you just crazy?" I immediately raised my hands and said, "Crazy." We both laughed. We talked for several hours and afterwards, we shared a mutual respect.

He told me, "When you finish basic training, they will ask for volunteers for Airborne School. You need to go. After Airborne

School, they will look for volunteers for Ranger School. You need to go. After that, you need to go to Cologne, Panama for Jungle Expert training, then to Alaska for cold weather training. When you have finished all of that, there is a fairly new outfit at Fort Bragg, North Carolina called the Special Forces; I have a feeling that is where you belong." He had just laid out the next years of my life. We became close friends and I had a tremendous amount of respect for that Sergeant.

FIRST LEAVE

After basic training, I got my first leave to go home. I went to Memphis to visit Mom and my sister for two weeks, but I never mentioned what was in store for me next. For a little while I fell back into my other life. I ran into my cousin Richard who had joined the Navy and was home on leave.

Richard and I had kind of grown up together. He had been invited to a party, so he invited me to go with him. He told me he had learned how to make a unique punch but that I should not drink it. We did not have much money, but we stopped by a store and Richard bought several items and off we went to the party. I was having a great time when someone came up to me and said, "Your friend needs your help. He thinks he is a termite that is trying get into the woodwork." "What?" I exclaimed. Richard had been drinking his own punch and was really messed up.

There was about two inches of snow on the ground so I took Richard outside and laid him out in the snow on his back thinking the snow would bring him around. That did not work so I hit him in the stomach. Everything exploded out of his mouth – he looked like an oil gusher. The problem was it all came back down on top of him.

All the girls turned on me; they felt like I had been mean to Richard. Using the snow, I tried to clean him up as best I could, and I put him in the trunk of my car to take him home with me. Whenever I brought a friend home, they always slept on the hide-a-bed in the living room. I undressed Richard on the porch down to his underwear then took him in the house and laid him out on the hide-a-bed. The next morning, I woke up listening to my sister and my mother laughing at Richard. I have to admit he did look rather comical laid out on the hide-a-bed in his underwear. I checked to make sure he was still breathing. He was, so we left him alone until about noon. Richard was one sick puppy. He was a living testament to the fact that you should never drink "Richard's Magic Punch."

AIRBORNE AND RANGER

Now it was about time for me to become the other me, the Sergeant in the Army, so I reported to Fort Benning Georgia for Jump School. Jump School was not that big of a deal – you only had to jump out of a plane five times and you could earn your wings; it was only two weeks of training and most of it was physical.

On my first three jumps, I did not have a problem because I was back in the line or stick as they call it. You just shuffle forward and before you know it you are in the door and out of the plane. No big deal.

My fourth jump, I was the first man in line, so I had plenty of time to look out the door. We were way up there, and I had way too much time to think, so I decided not to jump. Just as I was turning around to tell the Jumpmaster my decision, the light came on, and he kicked me out the door – so much for not jumping. When you stop and think about it, it does not make any sense to jump out of a perfectly good airplane. People say that only two things come out of the sky, bird droppings, and damn fools. Over the next 5 years, I jumped 181 times, proving without a shadow of a doubt which one I am.

Ranger school was by far my biggest challenge. You are pushed very hard to see if you would give up and quit. <u>Quitters do not Rangers make</u>. You never walk anywhere, you run, your arms ache from hundreds of push-ups, your brain aches from all the classes, and sleep deprivation was the name of the game of the day.

When in basic training, I had studied transcendental meditation. It is a method of conditioning yourself to go into a deep sleep for fifteen to twenty minutes and wake up totally refreshed. When you get a normal eight hours of sleep, you spend most of that time going into and coming out of a deep sleep. You only spend about fifteen to twenty minutes in deep sleep and that is where the real rest occurs. It takes a lot of practice, but transcendental meditation can give you a lot of control over yourself.

There is a segment of ranger school called 'sleep deprivation.' For twenty-one days they program your time to be busy twenty hours every day. That leaves you only four hours for all of your personal needs, including sleep. Those four hours may be split into two separate two-hour periods of time. About the third day tempers began to become short and everyone's tongue seemed to be sharp. About halfway through the second week, we lost most of the ones we would lose.

Those of us who had studied transcendental meditation had an easier time. There were some of the guys that just toughed it through. Think about this, you are tired, sleepy, and irritable. You are put in a classroom and told the instructor will be in shortly, but stay awake and alert. The room begins to get warmer and sleep is almost inevitable. You dose off and some joker slaps you in the back of the head real hard and screams at you. What is your reaction? Yes, me too. But living through that kind of thing is what makes a ranger able to do all of the many things normal people cannot do. Never call a ranger normal, because normal is average and average is as close to the bottom as it is to the top. No ranger has ever been close to the bottom of anything. He will be at the top or very close to it, or he will not be at all.

We spent time in mountains and swamps alike; We learned how to fight; and how to kill. We also learned how to cover long distances at night with our eighty-pound pack on our back, a map and a compass. We never went anywhere without that gear. We learned how to live off the land; we learned teamwork – "all for one and one for all," and we learned how to handle snakes.

Now in Roy's dictionary, look up the word snake and the word dead is always next to it. You do not see snake; you see the two words 'Dead Snake.' Roy does not like snakes. One of the guys, Roger I believe his name was, had a big mouth on an occasion and he picked up on the fact that some of us had a fear of snakes. He liked to laugh at us when we handled poisonous snakes. A couple of us got together and found a five-foot black snake and put it in Roger's bed under the covers.

One of the funniest things I have ever seen in my life was when Roger went to bed. He went in feet first and the snake became active and began to flop around. Roger's heartbeat went up substantially. It was not a good experience for Roger or the snake. We thought Roger would have a heart attack and I do not believe the snake liked the smell of urine. That's right; Roger urinated all over everything while he was trying to get away from the snake. I believe Roger got bit two or three times during the process, but it was a non-poisonous snake. A non-poisonous snake can be like a ghost – a ghost cannot hurt you – but he can make you hurt yourself. I can hardly write this for laughing. It was absolutely the funniest thing I have ever seen in my life. Roger dropped out of school the next morning.

When you see someone with a Ranger patch on his uniform, he deserves your respect. Somehow, I made it through school and was proud as a peacock when I had earned my Ranger patch.

JUNGLE SCHOOL

Now I was in the best shape of my life, 6 foot 2 inches tall 210 lbs. of romping, stomping hell. Time to go to Panama and Jungle School.

We arrived in Cologne, Panama for training. It was our first time to ever play in the jungle. They had a zoo with most of the animals you would find in the South American jungle. Because there are so many different kinds of snakes in the jungle, they wanted us to play with snakes a lot. I do not like snakes. They are okay to eat but not as playmates.

One of the survival exercises they put us through was to take three of us out in a helicopter about 20-25 miles and drop us off - no food, no water, no weapons. All we had was a knife and a compass and a rough map of the area. We were dropped off and told that if you made it back alive, we will go to our next area of training. We heard them laughing as the helicopter pulled away.

In one way of thinking twenty-five miles was not that far, but if you were out in the jungle twenty-five miles can be a journey into eternity. We were dropped off in late afternoon and had to get organized fast. Shelter for the night was our first concern, water and food were second and third. We located a very large tree with a small stream nearby and made our shelter about twenty feet high in the tree. This would keep us away from the ground dwelling animals. When it got dark in the jungle, it got dark fast. The sounds in the jungle are the scariest in the world, especially at night. Nothing sounded like what it was. A tree frog can sound like something with 6-inch teeth that is hungry.

I remember an old-timer telling me that it was not the animals that made all the noise that will get you, it is the ones that you didn't hear that will kill you. A not so comforting thought. We spent a listless night trying to sleep but to no avail. The night sounds do not let up until dawn. Then there are a whole new set of sounds to worry you. At dawn, we set out on our journey back to what we called civilization. Fighting our way through vines and sharp-edged grass, we kept an eye on our compass while hoping that we were going the right direction.

About noon, we came to a small river that looked about chest deep. It looked like we would be able to walk across it. One of the guys who had wandered off a distance came running back all excited and said, "You have to see this snake I found. He has to be the biggest snake in the world." That was the last thing I wanted to see, but we followed him a short distance up the river. There was a large snag sticking out of the water and coiled all over that snag was the biggest snake I have ever seen in my life – an anaconda. He looked to be thirty or forty feet long and was much larger around in the middle then I was. In reality, it was probably eighteen to twenty feet long, but still a huge snake.

My two idiot buddies were all excited and said, "Let's catch it and take it back for the zoo." I said, "Let me make this perfectly clear, 'Lets' is not going to mess with that snake. If you want to, you guys can catch it and I will build a cage to carry it." They devised a plan to get some pliable vines and fashion a noose on one end. Then they would climb the tree and go tree-to-tree until they were over the snake. At that point they planned to drop the noose down and let it touch the snake. When he raised his head, they would flip the noose over his head and pull up hard, tying the vine on to a tree limb and let the snake thrash around until he ran out of energy. Next, they would lower him into the cage. It sounded so simple, but it was not realistic.

When the noose was lowered, it touched the snake awaking him and he slid off into the river. It was at that point that I realized we had not crossed the river yet. How stupid can you be? We had to cross the river and I had just watched the biggest snake in the world slide into it. So, I headed out into the water and about halfway across something brushed my leg. It could have been a fish or a stick but in my mind, it was that huge snake going to get even for being disturbed. I know I had to look like a duck taking off as I splashed crazily to get across that river to the other side. I finally made it. When my two idiots came out of the water, I grabbed them both by the throat and made one thing clear. I had the knife and if they so much as talked about catching a mouse, I would kill them both and feed them to the snake.

We found some birds eggs and a limited amount of fruit to eat. We spent another night in the jungle and late the next afternoon, we made it back.

The next day we were to do our POW training. They had set up a Prisoner of War camp a couple of miles from the main training facility. They loaded about twenty of us as POWs into a truck and drove us over to the camp. They were calling the roll as we were jumping off the back of the truck. As I jumped off, I heard my name called and answered "Present." When I hit the ground among all of the confusion, I quickly crawled under the truck and crawled into the space made for the drive shaft. When the truck left, I was on top of the drive shaft trying to keep it off my chest but there was very little space. Well, the next 10 minutes or so I had to painfully tolerate that thing spinning against my body. When the truck stopped, I got loose, fell to the ground, crawled out from under the truck, and went to the main office and reported that I had escaped.

The commandant did not believe me until he saw the very large bruise that went from my neck down across my body to my crotch. He called the POW camp asked if anyone was missing. They said no, so he asked to speak to Sergeant Jones. After a few minutes, they told him they could not find me. I spent the next two days trying to recover from that horrible bruise. There were a great number of other things that we did in Jungle School, none of which were a whole lot of fun.

Camouflage and concealment was an area in which I seemed to excel. Even with my large size, I pulled it off. On one occasion, I was hidden in the leaves when an instructor, who I did not particularly like, walked by my position. He had been very vocal about he could not be fooled by camouflage, but he did not see me! I reached out and grabbed him by the ankle, pulling him to the ground. He screamed like a little girl and I could swear, just for a moment, I could smell the faint odor of ammonia. Yes, I think he wet himself. Everyone had a great laugh. The next day was our final day, and we hid and some of the guys were supposed to find us. Just like a big boy "Hide and Seek." The instructor from the day before walked by me and dumped about half a cup of ants on top of me as he passed. Now in my mind that is a killing offence. If I fail this part of the course, I will fail the school. I laid as still as I could with 100s of ants crawling all over my body and being bitten by some of them. The biggest problem was my eyes, ears, and nose. If ever you want to torture someone, put them in this situation. When the whistle blew and the exercise was over, I was the first one in the stream. Now I was ready to fight, school or no school graduation. My head instructor and several others grabbed me, while other cadre hustled that joker away. The head instructor had seen him dump the ants on me and everyone was amazed that I did not jump up. I guess you could say I learned something about myself that day and what I could endure.

There were a great number of other things that we did in Jungle School, but none more fun than that one last night when we were allowed to go into town. I vaguely remember strong drinks, pretty girls, police officers with short night sticks- a lot of pleasure, and pain. What a night!

SECOND LEAVE

Now it was time to take a short leave and go back home to Memphis. Back in Memphis, I could not bring myself to talk about what I had been through, so when questioned about it, I always answered, "Just off playing soldier." There was a young lady named Rita Watkins whom I had dated some while in school. She was involved with someone else at this time. I had been kind of adopted by her parents, so I spent some time with them. Her father had worked for the railroad and retired after 30 years. He did not drink but for many years when the holidays came, he was given liquor as a holiday gift. He had a closet literally stuffed with fifths of liquor; he did not know what to do with it, so he gladly gave me a number of bottles when I asked for them.

I scouted out some apartment complexes located near Memphis State University looking for the ones that might have housed the most college girls. About 6:30 or 7 o'clock I would take two bottles of liquor and go knocking on a door. When someone answered I would say, "Randy invited me to the party," and hold up two bottles of liquor. "Party, what party?" They would say. "There is no party." So, with a goofy smile on my face, I would hold up the two bottles of liquor and say, "Would you like to start one?"

I never had to knock on more than three doors before I had a party started. Sometimes before the evening was over the entire complex was involved in a big ole fun party. Most of the complexes had swimming pools so there we were, everyone in swimsuits but me. Someone always had access to music and off we went.

Here I am, again, that other person, a million miles away from jungles and snakes, enjoying just being me. There were always plenty of pretty ladies, which by the way is one of my many vices. I tried to limit myself to starting no more than three parties per trip home. No sense wearing out a good thing. No commitments or long-term relationships. That way, I did not have anyone back home worrying about me, which is the way I wanted it.

Roy could live life and have a good time without getting involved. Roy could be free. I have always been a little creative when it comes to finding entertainment. Starting a party with perfect strangers did not seem abnormal to me, and you got to meet a lot of pretty girls. I really enjoyed myself when I became Roy Jones, civilian, rather than Sergeant Jones. I never wore my uniform in Memphis. The uniform represented, to me, my other life, and I did not want to get them intertwined. But when you go home after being gone for a long time, what do you do? Your friends are all a little different and you are different. I found it's true, that you will change based on your personal experiences. Anytime you leave home for an extended period of time, you are slowly adjusting to your new surroundings, and becoming a little bit different in how you see and react to things. As this happens you slowly become a new person. I am a firm believer that you cannot ever "go home." Because the home you left behind is not the same today as it was when you left yesterday.

My way of living and thinking fits me perfectly. I have never felt the need to be entertained. I will take care of that myself with total strangers.

ALASKA

All fun times must come to an end, and it was time now to report to Fort Lewis, Washington as Sergeant Jones. We were taken by air to some place in Alaska for cold weather training. I do not like cold weather as I am a Tennessee boy. This school only lasted thirty days, 30 very long, very cold, days and nights. We were dropped off at a place, we were told, where the snow was never less than twenty feet deep. The instructors had nice warm tents and this thing called fire which creates heat, but we were deprived of all of this.

The first night, we slept on top of the snow. Every soldier had a canvas shelter half, or half a two-man tent commonly called a "pup tent." You spread out your shelter-half on the snow. On top of that, you spread out your poncho, then your blanket, then your sleeping bag. You fold over the bottom of the shelter-half then the two sides. You now have a cocoon. After taking off your boots you slide down into the cocoon and take all your clothes off. At this time, you would reach back and pull the last remaining point over your face to finish your cocoon, making sure to leave two breathing holes. You must take your clothes off to prevent sweating during the night. Sweat turns to ice and your warm body then melts the ice, which becomes very cold water. I was really surprised at how warm and cozy my rifle and I were during the night. I slept like a rock. All was wonderful until I flipped that top piece back in the morning and the four inches of snow that had fallen during the night came in to join me in my warm cocoon.

Let's see, snow, heat, water, ice – there is a combination for a Tennessee country boy. I had to get dressed in a hurry and shake the ice out of my cocoon. We were not allowed to go to the warm tents the instructors had, so I froze my butt off. I still do not like snow except on television. The second night, we dug a hole in the snow barely large enough for two men to sit facing one another. You would find a large piece of ice to cover your hole. Two men got into the hole facing one another. We would take our hands and run them slowly along the sides of the hole. Your body heat melts the snow which then turns to ice. This would keep the sides from caving in on you. After doing that, you would take your boots off, and put your feet under your buddy's armpits, and he put his feet under your armpits. That is how we slept after pulling the slab of ice over our hole. The third night, we learned how to make igloos and during the day we played War. No one froze to death, although we did have several minor cases of frostbite.

There were many things to consider when living in the cold and snow. How do you build a fire with frozen, wet wood and where would you build this fire even if you had matches? At some point you try to locate grass or leaves. You would stuff some between your shirt and field jacket after it had thawed out. Then you would have additional insulation and fire starter material. When you do get a fire built, you needed to remember when you put it out to take some charcoal to put in your pocket. Nothing is better for stomach problems than charcoal. It absorbs all of the poison in your system. Therefore, when you are out in the world, keep some charcoal in your pocket.

After four weeks of this madness, we were returned to Fort Lewis, Washington to thaw out. I talked to God and asked Him to please never again make me have to fight in that kind of weather. I have the utmost respect for our troops that regularly train to fight in that damn cold and snow. It takes a special kind of person to be able to do that, and I am not that special.

FORT LEWIS, WASHINGTON

We were given three days to acclimate at Fort Lewis, which meant, "Let's go to Seattle and play." Two of my buddies and I were in Seattle in one of the seedier parts of town when I spotted a sign in the window of a bar that said, "Dogs and G.I.s, keep out." Now, to my weird way of thinking, it said, "Welcome, come on in." We went in and after a few words with a manager, we were served, and he called the Military Police.

Two Military Police came in a short time later. They seemed to believe they were in charge, but we had different ideas. I noticed that they were wearing Class A uniforms with their boots bloused, and I did not see any Airborne wings on their uniforms. In the service at that time, the only two groups that could wear Class A Uniforms with their boots bloused were Airborne and Military Police.

I did not agree with their being able to dress that way. A heated discussion ensued and ended with us knocking out both of the police; I then took out my pocketknife and cut their boots off to make shoes out of them. When they woke up, they left in a big hurry. We kept drinking, but it was not long before they returned with what you might call a host of people. There were city police and a lot of military police. We were subdued and put in jail. The next day back at Fort Lewis, the Commanding General wanted me hung out by the main gate as an example. He was mad that I had embarrassed his MPs (Military Police) that way. There was a Special Forces Colonel there to take us to Fort Bragg and he convinced the General that he was more than capable of issuing the kind of punishment that we so richly deserved.

We loaded onto that big old jet and took off for Fort Bragg for testing to see if we could qualify to become part of the Special Forces. We were not in the air very long before the call went out, "Sergeant Jones, report to the Colonel." My heart dropped. I reported to the Colonel, and he stared at me for a long moment with a very stern look on his face, then he asked me, "Sergeant, do you have suicidal tendencies?" "No sir," I answered cautiously. He said, "Sergeant Jones, we are in an aircraft that is 40,000 feet up in the air and traveling at about 500 miles an hour. If I told you to parachute out of it right now would you do it?" I hesitated for a moment, and then said, "Yes sir, if you ordered me to, I would jump."

He stared at me for another long minute, and then in a very authoritative voice, he said, "Sergeant Jones, you are to consider yourself confined to the inside of this aircraft for the duration of the flight. Do you understand me, Sergeant?" I hesitated for just a moment before answering, "You do not want me to jump, is that it, Sir?" The Colonel said, "You have just been issued an Article 15 company punishment for your actions in Seattle, is that clear?" "Yes sir," I replied.

Then the Colonel broke out into a wide grin and said, "Sit down and tell me all about it. Did you really cut their boots off and make shoes out of them because they did not have airborne wings?" "Yes, sir," I said, and we sat and talked and laughed for about an hour. "You are my kind of soldier," he said, as I got up to go back to my seat.

SPECIAL FORCES SCHOOL

John F Kennedy, the 35th president of the United States, had a special place in his heart for the Special Forces, probably because he commanded a PT boat in the Second World War. The PT boats were known as mosquito boats because they were so fast. They could attack a large ship, doing a lot of damage, and be gone in a flash.

The chosen headgear for the Special Forces was a rifle green beret. The commanding general at Fort Bragg did not like them because it set the Special Forces apart. Thus, he issued an order outlawing the wearing of the beret. That did not mean they stopped wearing them – they just stopped wearing them when they were around other people. President Kennedy was to visit Fort Bragg and the problem with the beret was brought to his attention. He issued a presidential decree that the official head gear of the United States Special Forces was to be a Green Beret and that settled the matter for good.

The Special Forces was formed to initiate special operations around the world. Most of the operations were so secret, the specifics will never be known to the general public. They are highly trained in every aspect of warfare and are known for their quick-hit and gone tactics, and their ability to recruit and train local people to fight. My goal was to try to join this group of very special men. I will not delve into the specifics of the training except to say, if you are not of above-average intelligence, above-average physically; with an above-average commitment to excellence you will not be there for long. I would like to share with you a few of the lessons I learned that have served me well to this day.

Lesson 1: One of the instructors kept an aquarium in his office that was full of rattlesnakes. He took them to class one day and began by saying, "You see these snakes all well fed, warm and happy? They represent 99% of the organizations in the world. Now, see what happens when you introduce outside agitation." With that he took a stick and stirred them up. They started striking at anything that moved, including each other. "Like most humans when they feel threatened, they strike at and blame each other rather than evaluating the threat and dealing with the actual cause. If you are like the snakes, you need to leave this program right now. Here, we are more like the buffalo and the musk oxen. If you put a pack of wolves on to a herd of buffalo, they will do the same thing every time. They will circle up with the horns out and the weak, old, and young in the middle of the circle. As long as none of them panics, they are invincible. That is the way of the Green Beret. We circle up and protect the group from all threats, no matter what they are. We go out on missions together. We all come back together - dead or alive. One unit acting as one person." That has been my philosophy from that day until this day. When I am building a team, I will not tolerate anyone who does not fully support the team. Together we win; as individuals we fail. 'Superman does not exist.'

Lesson 2: One bright sunny morning, we were told we were going on a 50-mile run. Not in t-shirts, shorts and special running shoes, but with full 80 lb. packs on our back and wearing combat boots. We would run for 50 minutes, walk for 10 minutes, run for 50 minutes, then rest for 10 minutes, then begin all over again until we had covered 50 miles. We would be given fresh canteens of water on the 10-minute rest periods. Now if that doesn't sound too hard give it a try. If you are trying to escape to the border of a foreign country, you need to know you have what it takes to succeed.

At some point, probably about halfway, one of the guys grabbed his side and fell into the ditch and a very large instructor jumped into the ditch with him screaming at him, calling him names and threatening him. He made that soldier more afraid of him than he was of God. When the solider came out of the ditch, some of us shared his load so he could finish the run. One of the things that kept me going was thinking, if I fell in the ditch and that joker jumped on top of me, he had better never go to sleep again because I would see that he did not wake up. After the run, we went straight into a classroom. The instructor asked, "What did we learn today? What I hope you learned was that when you have gone as far as you think you can go, you are exactly halfway to where you are capable of going if properly motivated. When your mind and your body are on the same wavelength, you can perform what normal people call "superhuman acts." This is another lesson that has stayed with me. Many times, I was so tired that I would sit down and say, "Surely, I am at least halfway." All I was sure of was, I couldn't quit."

Lesson 3: The seven Ps – Proper Planning and Preparation Prevents Pitifully Poor Performance. Doing an exhaustive amount of planning and preparation for a mission could well mean the difference between success and failure, life or death. Always have a plan, plan A, plan B and plan C. Everyone in the team knows the plan. If things do not go well, you just say, "Go to plan B," and everyone knows what to do. A team is acting as one person. There will be times when something unforeseeable will happen, and you have to make it up as you go along to survive. By doing the seven P's, it does not happen often, but it does happen.

Later in life when I got into the business world, my nickname was Mr. Lucky and I wore a name tag with Mr. Lucky on it. Many people doing the same or similar job that I was doing seemed to have a lot of mountains to climb. Being a planner, I had it easier than most of them. By doing the seven P's, I had figured out there was a path through the valleys between the mountains. Most of the people I worked with would not listen and never seemed to understand.

The seven P's work in every part of your life. Planning your spiritual life is very important, planning time to study your Bible, or prayer time and time to go to church – all of this requires planning. Even taking your girlfriend out on a date requires planning. It works. This strategy became second nature to me and still does.

These three lessons are just a small sample of what I have learned, but they stand out in my mind. At one point after a lot of the guys had washed out or quit, they issued each one of us a dog. We were to shoot the dog with a 22 rifle, not to kill him but to wound him and as part of our medical training we were to nurse the dog back to health. If your dog died, you failed. Not long after I finished the course, the ASPCA became aware of what was happening and stopped that part of the training. It is my contention that you can talk about sewing flesh and treating infection all you want to but there is no substitute for the real thing. There is no better training in the world than that of the United States Special Forces, The Navy Seals might come close. Of the 80 men that started the training cycle, three of us were awarded the coveted Green Beret.

In the mid 60s, after I was out of the Army, SSG Barry Sadler wrote a song that became very poplar called "Ballad of the Green Beret. The song was so concise and to the point it brought goose bumps to my arms. The song went like this:

>Fighting Soldiers from the sky,
>
>>Fearless men who jump and die;
>
>Men who mean just what they say
>
>>The brave men of the Green Beret;
>
>Silver wings upon their chest
>
>>These are men America's best
>
>100 men will test today
>
>>But only 3 win the Green Beret

Trained to live off nature's land

      Trained in combat hand-to-hand

Men who fight by night and day

      Courage taken from the Green Beret

Silver Wings upon their chest

      These are men America's best

100 men will test today,

      But only 3 win the Green Beret

Back at home a young wife waits

      Her Green Beret has met his fate

He has died for those oppressed

      Leaving her with his last request.

Put Silver Wings on my son's chest

      Make him one of America's best

He'll be a man they'll test one day

      Have him win the Green Beret.

SSG Sadler did a great job capturing the essence of the Green Beret in very simple terms.

In the spring of 1961, The President activated the 5th Special Forces Group and I was assigned to an A team to began training with them. One thing that never stopped was training. On one exercise, we were positioned on top of a high hill with a company of Airborne troops at the bottom of the hill. After dark they were to move up the hill and capture us. Our mission was to move down the hill and get past them. Twelve men at the top, fifty men at the bottom – sounds about even to me.

While we are waiting for it to get dark, it occurred to us that a breeze was blowing down the hill. So, after some discussion, we built a bonfire and most of the guys danced around it like complete idiots. We distracted those at the bottom of the hill while three guys collected poison ivy and poison oak. Quickly, we all put on our gas masks before throwing the poison ivy and poison oak onto the fire, which created a tremendous amount of smoke which then rolled like an avalanche down that hill.

We stayed back from the fire avoiding the smoke, and it was only a short time before the people at the bottom of the hill were having serious eye and lung problems. A fair number of them were taken to the hospital, and we escaped in the confusion. Now the ones that were supposed to be good guys seemed to be upset with us, as they thought we had done a bad thing. But we were trying to win and did.

An Airborne Major came into our area to find the person responsible for that stunt. He decided that it was entirely my fault and was talking about a court-martial when my Colonel arrived. He explained that we were an unconventional warfare unit and we did not like games. We did not think like normal soldiers. He explained to the Major that perhaps his children should play with someone their own age. This was the same Colonel I had met on the plane. Before he left, he looked directly at me, smiled, and gave me a knowing wink.

VIET NAM – FIRST TRIP

A quick response alert was called. This meant you would grab your always packed bag and run to the airfield. We boarded a large plane and took off. Usually we would fly around for an hour or so then land and be chewed out for being too slow. This time we did not land but kept flying. After another hour or two it became obvious that we were on a real mission. The mood in the plane changed and everyone became very serious. The officers were up in the front of the plane planning. After refueling in the air, we flew for about fifteen more hours; we landed in Thailand and were spirited away to a special area away from the airport. This is where we learned we were going to Viet Nam, "The flower of the orient".

In the United States, there are basically four venomous snakes- the coral snake, cottonmouth, copperhead and a variety of rattlesnakes. You rarely hear of anyone dying from being bitten by these.

Viet Nam there is 37 different kinds of venomous snakes including some of the deadliest in the world. One of these is the King Cobra, which grows to be about 18 feet long. This snake can stand up one third of its body length. Jack, Nim, and I ran into one of these on one of the patrols we did. We came close to "her" nest and she stood up to look Jack eye-to-eye with her hood filled out. It must have been a foot wide. All of us went into shock. There she was about 10 feet in front of Jack, and He was in shock. On instinct, I quickly empted a clip from my AK47 into her. When Jack recovered, he emptied his clip. The shock of it scared all of us. All of a sudden, there she is standing up right in front of you- eye to eye. Nightmares are born at such moments. Jack had a problem sleeping for a long time, and It affected me for a week of so.

Along with the snakes, there is a 100 leg centipede that is venomous. This thing eats bats. Then there are tigers, wolves and crocodiles round out most of the animals in Viet Nam. A lot of things over there want to kill you and some of them want to eat you.

Welcome, this will be your home for the next year. Should you survive you will not be the person you are today. You will change as you learn to survive.

How do you prepare men to face all of this, and still do the job you trained them to do? You start with mental toughness, you select only men that are mentally tough and think outside of the box. You make these men to survive any circumstance.--"Confront, Adapt and Overcome" became the slogan, and becomes a way of life for them. These "Special Forces" men will give you all they have to give all day and every day.

We spent several days planning. There were five teams and a command group. We were to be deployed to build camps in the mountains of Northern South Vietnam. My team was dropped off on top of a large hill in the middle of nowhere. There were several Montagnard villages within a couple of miles of our position. The Montagnard, or Mountain people, wanted to be left alone and to live in peace. These people were very family oriented and very small in stature. Their physical size did not determine the size of their hearts. They were great people and I fell in love with them. They would chew betelnut, so their teeth were always black; to them a sign of beauty was to have your teeth ground down to a nub. These people wore loin cloths and carried crossbows; they were about five feet tall and weighed about 80 pounds. But I would take one of them over five regular Vietnamese in a fight.

We visited the villagers and offered them money to help build our camp. Their question to us was, "What is money?" They had no idea. We finally reached an accommodation with them to trade goods for work. The CIA ferried building materials and equipment for us. One of the "yards," as we called them, named Nim adopted me during the construction process. I had picked him up just as he was about to step on a very venomous snake. No big deal, what you would do for anyone. Before I knew it, Nim had set up near the team house and lived there. Nim hated the North Vietnamese with a passion. He collected ears, that's right, I said ears. Whenever he killed a North Vietnamese, he would cut off his left ear and put it on a stringer. His collection was well over 100 ears when I met him. A dried-out ear resembled a prune. Nim had watched from the jungle as the North Vietnamese murdered his father, mother, brothers and sisters. That was the understandable basis for his hate.

In Vietnam, there were no great weather days. It was hot and humid. But from a helicopter, one could see some of the most beautiful country in the world. I would say the average person who went to the country lost 10 to 20 percent of his body weight in the first 45 days. It is like living in a sauna and it sapped your energy. When you hear the phrase 'hot as hell', this is the place they are talking about. You would suffer from what we called "Jungle Rot." Your skin would peel off in pieces-mostly on your feet and hands. I had been out of the service for eight years before I got rid of mine.

We were attached to the CIA and regularly sent on missions. I could not count the number of times that I found myself in North Vietnam, Cambodia and Laos; but it did not really matter because we were not 'officially' there anyway. We were part of a group that was to do "black ops" (black operations) and do "wet work" (assassinations) when necessary.

I will never forget the first time I knowingly killed a man.

It was early on my first tour, on my first mission with two other guys. It was supposed to be a LRRP, or Long Range Reconnaissance Patrol. On a LRRP, you avoid contact with the enemy and observe the movements of men and material, then report back. That sounds great but it is not always possible. We were well hidden, and a bad guy actually stepped on Jack. Jack grabbed him, pulled him down and was wrestling with him when another enemy came around the tree.

I threw my throwing hatchet as hard as I could and hit him in the side of the head. I didn't even think, I just reacted. For a long time, I had been practicing throwing at targets and trees, but this was the first time I had thrown at a man and killed him. Jack won his match with the other foe and did it with his knife. I went to retrieve my hatchet and it was lodged in his skull. It was a horrible sight! I had to work at it to get it dislodged. I was in a daze but charged with adrenaline as I stared into what was left of his face. It made me sick. Jack brought me back to reality. We had to hide those two bodies and get out of there. We had to move fast and put some distance between us and them. In case they tried to follow us, we decided to go a different direction and then circle back to the direction we needed to go. Just as I came around a large tree, I ran into another enemy guy. He hit me in the upper left chest real hard with the butt of his rifle just as I jammed my thumb into his eye. I grabbed my hatchet, raised it high above my head and came down with all my might diagonally across his body almost cutting him in half.

We had stumbled upon a small group of enemy fighters bedding down for the night. The one I had killed was an outpost sentry. We could not afford to start a shooting fight because we were not supposed to be there. We evidently did not cause an alarm, so we safely beat it out of there. We had to move fast, but at night that is really difficult to do without making a lot of noise. We found a trail going the right direction and decided to risk taking it. One more time, God was holding his protective hand over me.

We followed the trail for most of the night to put as much

distance as possible between us and them. When the sun began to come up, we hid out well off the trail to rest. I couldn't sleep and took the first watch. Every time I closed my eyes, I saw the face of the first guy I had killed. About noon, we started moving again staying off the trails. It took two more days to get back to camp and report in. The Captain was not pleased that we had left bodies all over the jungle, as he put it. As for me, I was just happy to be alive, a twenty-year-old boy- 10,000 miles from home and surrounded by people who want to kill you.

On one occasion, I was sent with some South Vietnamese soldiers (Army Republic Vietnam Nation – ARVN) into enemy territory. We were ambushed. I was up front with their scout running point when it happened. All hell broke loose. The South Vietnamese soldiers immediately fell back and left me out in the jungle alone. They all ran away led by their Captain. I found myself lying under some brush near a trail. I could see the feet of the Viet Cong soldiers (the VC enemy) running up and down the trail looking for me. I could also hear the screams of several South Vietnamese who had been captured. I was scared to death. To make my situation worse, I saw a movement out of the corner of my eye. It was what we called a "Two Step Charlie." a very venomous snake. The name "Two Step" came from the knowledge that once bitten, you could take about two steps before you died.

Having only one shell left in my shotgun; I was in a real dilemma about what to do. I needed to reload but could not move without being discovered. Do I jump up and shoot the snake, then take my chances with the soldiers or, shoot at the Viet Cong and take my chances with two steps? I did the only thing I could do. I froze. "Two Step" kept coming until he reached my right hand that was on the trigger of a shotgun. He proceeded very slowly over my hand and the shotgun then across my left arm just above the wrist and kept going. "Two Step" was about 10 inches from my face, which made him look a lot larger than he actually was. I was so relieved when his tail dropped off my wrist; I wet myself. Now I have to move because the smell of urine in the jungle is an alien smell. If I stay where I am, they will surely smell me out. I began to back away very slowly crawling backwards until I was well out of sight of the trail.

I moved very slowly, but deliberately, until I was well away from that area. Now it was getting dark and I needed shelter for the night, but I couldn't make any noise. I did not know where the VC were located. Climbing way up into a large tree, I straddled a limb facing the trunk of the tree. I tied myself to the trunk of the tree to make sure I did not fall out during the night. My intention was to sleep, but sleep never came.

Here I am 20 years old, two weeks from my 21st birthday, 10,000 miles from home and lost in a foreign jungle with little people running around wanting to kill me. I had not felt that alone since I was in the hospital at St Peter's orphanage when I had my eye surgery. I sat there hugging the tree and crying all night long.

Morning finally came and I cautiously climbed down the tree, "Here I am" I said to myself, "a big baby. Yes, you're lost. Yes, you're far away from home. Yes, a lot of people want to hurt you. Yes, you can get mean and do what you were trained to do or die." Since I had cried all night long, my eyes hurt, I was still lost, and far away from home. Since nothing had been solved by the crying, I swore I would never cry again. This is another one of those times that God was holding his protective hand over me. I do not know why He loves me so much, but He surely does.

After traveling a day and a half, I began to recognize some of the country around me. Then all of a sudden; I knew where I was and where the camp was located. I made my way back to our camp. But you do not just walk up the trail and into the camp without getting shot. I had been gone for three days. I hid along the trail that I knew they would be taking to go out and set up night ambush. After the first part of the patrol went by, I grabbed the last man while talking very loudly. It worked; no one was injured.

The patrol radioed the camp that I was alive and coming in. Word went out that I was alive, and that South Vietnamese Captain took his men and slipped out the back of the camp, never to return. He was lucky he heard that I was coming in, because I was looking for him with blood in my eye. They had reported that I had been killed and they had lost six men of their own.

I never trusted another South Vietnamese soldier after that episode. My friends noticed that something had changed in me; 'The Fourth Person Within' was beginning to raise his ugly head. Even my best friend Jack Jackson asked me about the change. He said, "Roy, I see no gentleness in you, what happened?" So, I told him. Jack was my best friend; we were exactly alike except Jack was about an inch taller, and so black that he was almost blue. I let it be known that I would operate with the "yards" only – no South Vietnamese soldiers because it would not be safe for them to go out with me.

One of the things people rarely hear about in Vietnam is the presence of tigers. Yes, I said TIGERS. The tiger is a native species to that part of the world, but most people never see them. Seeing a tiger in a zoo is one thing, but when you see one in the wild it is terrifying. I only saw tigers on two occasions. They were huge and fast. A full-grown tiger can grab a full-grown man in its mouth and run with him.

It was very dark late at night; you were with a small group of three people. You could hear a tiger roar in the distance; you knew he could see in the night, but you could not. This is what nightmares are made of in the jungle.

If you got involved in a firefight, the tigers in the area go toward the shooting instead of running away, because they know, when the shooting stops, they can feed. That is a very unsettling thought. In spite of the tigers and the fact that snakes were more active at night, that is when we did our best work.

I recently had a visit with an Army Chaplain who was in Viet Nam and he told me about being in a hospital visiting one of the men who had been on late night guard duty. A tiger had grabbed him and took off. The men would not shoot at the tiger because they could hit the soldier. When the tiger jumped a ravine, he dropped the man and the men let go with all they had but they missed the tiger. The man he grabbed was severely injured but lived. I cannot even imagine what that man has since gone through mentally.

The CIA wanted us to go to a certain area and bring back prisoners to interrogate. Jack and I were specialists in Long Range Reconnaissance Patrols, so we drew the mission. Nim always went with us, and this time we also took a guy named Greenlaw. We felt like four was the magic number since we needed to bring back two men. There were very few helicopters available in country at that time and we were going into other countries, so we had to walk everywhere we went.

On a mission like this, you travel mostly at night and stay off the trails, so travel is very slow, at best. After a three- or four-day walk, we arrived at the area they had designated, which was in another country. Next, now we had to find a small group of enemy soldiers. After a good while, we located a group of five men. That meant we had to kill three and take two back, but we had to do it very quietly. No shooting and always going for the throat. Most people have seen in the movies where someone gets stabbed and falls down dead. That is not really how it happens. There is always a lot of screaming and noise that goes along with being stabbed unless you cut the throat.

The plan was Nim was going to kill one and then help Jack. Jack was going to kill one and grab one. Greenlaw was going to grab one and I was going to kill one and backup Greenlaw. The two we were to take back had to be knocked out. Sounds simple, but remember it is all done with a knife to the throat. The best laid plans sometimes do not work the way they should. Greenlaw got cut pretty bad but he did not make any noise. Those that were supposed to die- died; and those that were supposed to live, lived.

I had used my Bowie knife which is very efficient for that kind of work. I had to sew up Greenlaw with a piece of steel wire that I carried just for that purpose. We now had two prisoners and one wounded man. We built a litter and I made the prisoners understand they were to carry the litter, and if they were not gentle, Nim would cut off their ears.

'The Fourth Person Inside' was now taking over my life. I was becoming someone who I did not recognize. We walked for two days before we reached the extraction point. Two helicopters came, one for Greenlaw and one for the two prisoners. Greenlaw did survive and I saw him about six weeks later. I was so upset at what happened to Greenlaw that I got on the helicopter with the prisoners, I wanted to make sure they told us what they knew. Through an interpreter I began to question one of the prisoners. He refused to talk. He would just look at me and shake his head no. Evidently, we had a 'Good Guy' reputation with the bad guys, but at this point I was not a good guy.

Eventually, I became frustrated and grabbed the one I had been questioning. I held him out of the door and turned to the interpreter and asked him if he really believed that I would not drop him. I looked at him he shook his head no and I let him go. Big mistake on his part. I let him go and I quickly grabbed the other one and stuck him out the door and asked him. Still hearing the first one screaming on the way to the ground. The second guy's head was shaking up and down like a bobblehead on the dashboard of a 57 Chevrolet, to show that he believed. I pulled him back inside. 'The Fourth Person Within' was now firmly in control.

We arrived back at the CIA camp and there was a regular Army "Light" (Lt) Colonel (LTC) there with them. Everyone wanted to know why there was only one prisoner, when we had picked up two. I told them he had tried to escape and fell out of the helicopter, which sounded simple to me. The Lt. Colonel did not like my answer, so he questioned everyone who had been on the helicopter. Since they had heard my answer, they all told the same story.

I don't know why that "Light" Colonel (LTC) was there, but it became very evident that he did not like the Special Forces. He got in my face and said, "I know you murdered that man and if I could prove it, you would be on your way to Leavenworth, now get back up there in the mountains with the rest of those animals where you belong." "Everyone belongs somewhere," I said, and I invited him, "Come visit sometime," and with a chuckle I turned and left. I could have passed a lie detector test at that very moment because I did not see myself as having killed that man. All I did was turn him loose, but I would be willing to bet that sudden stop in the jungle probably messed him up a bit. We were flying at about 8,000 feet.

There were a fair number of regular army people who did not like us, mostly because they did not understand us and our mission. Some thought we lived on another planet and just visited here to remind them the only reason they could stay on earth was because we tolerated them. I have heard this said out loud, but not by us.

We had a different purpose in life and a different view of life and death. We did not think like what you call 'normal people.' I guess the term unconventional warfare specialist says it all.

Later, one of the CIA guys told me the man I brought back was an officer and shared a treasure trove of information. Anytime he would slow down giving up the information, they would ask him if they needed to go get that Sergeant that brought him back. He would start talking again because he was terrified of me.

As a result of our success with that one officer, the CIA developed a new way of interrogation. They would put a prisoner in a helicopter, then blindfold him, take off, all the while asking him questions. The helicopter would ease back down until it was about 2 feet off the ground. If the person interrogated became uncooperative, he would throw him out the door. In the prisoner's mind, he was way up high, but he only fell a few feet. They would take the blindfold off and go to about 5,000 feet and hold him out the door then bring him back in. They always got the answers they were after.

Remember, this is in the late 50s and early 60s and we would not tolerate any team member taking any mind-altering chemicals, including marijuana. I only know of one case where a team member was caught taking drugs. He was warned, but he did not stop. His team went out on a mission and everyone came back alive but him. The thought of someone backing me up with that crap in their system scared me to death, as it did anyone else. Remember there were two to twelve men acting as one at all times. There is no room for anyone who might break down. All we had when we are on mission is each other. If you hurt, I hurt. That is just the way it is.

Our goal was to build a 200-man Strike Force (paid soldiers-Mercenaries). We recruited mountain people "Yards" and South Vietnamese alike. The CIA gave us money to pay them so to them it was like being in the regular army. One of the ways we acquired some of our people was to go to the local jail and buy them from the local law enforcement- Sheriff. We would tell them they were now in our army and would be paid every two weeks. We made it clear that if they gave us any trouble or ran off, we would hunt them down and kill them. We only had to hunt down two of them. 'The Fourth Person Within' was now in total control of everything I did.

One night between missions, we were trying to relax in the team Hooch when we heard a lot of shouting and laughing outside. We went out to see what was going on; The "Yards" had captured a male Gibbon monkey and killed a female monkey. They cut the female parts out of her and were taunting the male monkey with them. He was all worked up going crazy in the cage. They then took a chicken and rubbed the female parts all over the rear end of the chicken. They threw the chicken in the cage with the male monkey and all hell broke loose. That male monkey finally caught the chicken and tried to have sex with it.

The site of all that turned my stomach but I did not stop it. I had to remember that I was in a foreign country with completely different beliefs and customs from mine. This is what these people called entertainment and was normal for them. There is no way I could force my values on these people and make it stick. Eventually they ate both monkeys and the chicken. I never enjoyed eating monkey. It tasted bitter and it looked like a baby on a stick over the fire. I preferred snake or one of the other animals we could catch out of the camp. At our main camp we had access to Korean War C rations.

While on a mission, we could not carry anything that could identify us as American soldiers, so no canned food or rations. I do not remember ever seeing an overweight GI the whole time I was over there.

I did learn a lot about catching monkeys. You would get something like an empty coconut shell and cut a small hole in one end and a larger hole in the other. A vine would be run through the larger hole, then the smaller hole with a knot on the end so it could not come out of the smaller hole. Tie it to a tree and put a few rocks in the shell. Then stand there and shake it making a rattling noise. When you laid it down and walked away, the monkeys would be all over it shaking it and looking in the hole. One of them would put his hand in the hole and grab the rocks. At that point you could walk up and kill it with a stick. He would not let go of the rocks to get his hand out.

The Yards would put a mild poison on the tip of their arrow and wrap a small rag around it and shoot a monkey way up in the trees. The monkey would scream, look down and see the rag sticking out and try to poke it back in, - like it was his insides. Then he died from the poison and fell out of the tree. That is so smart because if you just shoot the monkey he will take off through the trees and probably die somewhere else. I don't know how they figured that one out, but when you stop and think about it, it's a brilliant thing to do. I learned a lot from the "Yards" and have a tremendous amount of respect for them as a people.

One of our teams had gone out on a mission and did not return when they should have. There were a great many things that could happen to make them late returning. After all, we were operating in enemy territory. The Captain sent Jack, Nim, and me out to look for them. It was like looking for a needle in a haystack; we almost never used trails and that was a very large jungle.

At the end of our second day, we found them – or what was left of them. They had been mutilated and you could tell by their body parts they had been tortured to death and then beheaded. Their heads were missing. The way we identified them was by their skin color and clothes. I had never seen anything like that in my worst nightmares. Their fingers had been cut off at the first knuckle. Their knees had been smashed. It was a sight that will live with me until I die. I became depressed and enraged at the same time. We all got physically ill gathering up the body parts to put in plastic bags. This was the hardest thing I had ever done, and it took a toll on my sanity. 'The Fourth Person Within' wanted vengeance.

We took the remains back to camp and shared the bad news with the other team members. Our team had been reduced by one fourth in one fell swoop. The Captain asked us to hold our emotions in check until we could gather more information. We did not want to, but it made sense to take vengeance on the right people.

It took about two weeks before we got word about a large group that had been bragging and showing off three heads. They were about three miles on our side of the Cambodia border. We put a plan together to annihilate them. We split our forces; the Captain took most of our strike force along with three team members to form a blocking force just inside the Cambodian border. The Lieutenant, Jack, and I, along with Wilson and Nim, took about thirty strikers (mercenary soldiers) to form the attacking force.

We located the group of soldiers and set up for an attack at 3 in the morning. We split up into fifteen teams of two and spread out in a semicircle around one side. At exactly 3 a.m., we began killing with our knives and crossbows until the first shots were fired.

Then we all attacked with a vengeance. Total panic ensued and most of them broke and ran for the border, running right into our other force that was waiting for them. It was a slaughter. I don't believe any of them got away. There were about one hundred and fifty of them.

At dawn, after making sure they were all dead, we set explosives in their supplies and prepared to leave. We blew up the supplies and left the bodies for the insects and animals. The heads of the six highest ranking officers were put on poles in the middle of the camp. The poles with heads on them stood in mute testimony to the fact that we could deal in terror as well. It was a solemn trip back to camp. Did this action even the score? NOT ON YOUR LIFE. One of our brothers' lives was worth thousands of theirs. This was just a down payment because they had taken the lives of three of our brothers in a most brutal way. As we left, we felt like we had walked up to and kicked down the "Gates of Hell" just to walk in and look around. We were not impressed.

News of our action got back to headquarters and the Captain was called in to explain our involvement in an unauthorized action. The Captain explained that we were on a training exercise and were attacked. Headquarters knew better and were trying to figure out how to explain the fact there were no wounded prisoners and the six heads on the poles. After much discussion they decided to bury the incident, and no one ever spoke of it again. 'The Fourth Person Within' was within all of us – including top brass.

I had been promoted to STAFF SERGEANT (SSG) on my first tour. In our outfit the only place rank meant anything was the pay line. They sent me back to the rear for a little rest and relaxation. There I sat. The only American in town in a bar with a lady on each knee, and a bottle in one hand when something inside of me clicked. 'The Fourth Person Within' arrived.

I looked around the room at all those people and wondered how many of these people are not on my side, which was a very bad place for my mind to go. I decided if there was one in there who was not on my side, I was going to get him. I stood up. Girls hit the floor and it began. During all the fighting that followed tables and chairs were thrown.

When things settled down and I found myself alone, I noticed a hole in the wall that led to another bar. I crawled through the hole and then it began again. When that room was settled, I found myself with the edge of a table trying to knock a hole into the mud wall to the next bar. I did not make the hole large enough and got stuck trying to crawl through it. When the police arrived, my head, one arm and shoulder were in one room and the rest of my body was in the other. I was beaten unmercifully with their sticks and put in jail. The next morning the American Commander had me picked up, and I found myself standing in front of a Major being screamed at.

He said, "The United States is spending $1,000,000 a day to promote goodwill with these people and you screw it all up in one night." I had a really bad headache and told the major, "If you are going to shoot me, shoot me now, but all of that screaming is not necessary." I was sent back up north with one less stripe. ` No big deal, my guys did not count stripes.

Jack, Nim, and I specialized in long range patrol. A lot of the time we were out we had to avoid contact, just observe and report back. However sometimes we were sent on a specific mission. Most of what we did was small scale by Army standards- not one large group fighting another large group. Our way was more one on one and we liked it that way because we had confidence in ourselves and each other. Don't misunderstand me, there were times we were outnumbered four or five to one but most of the time surprise was our biggest asset.

On one occasion, we observed a South Vietnamese company getting ambushed by a smaller group. It did not take long before the South Vietnamese were in a trap they could not escape. We decided to help them. We worked our way behind the enemy and began to take them out with our knives and Nim's crossbow. By the time they discovered we were there we had taken out ten or twelve of them. When the first shot was fired, we attacked. They had no way of knowing how many of us there were, and they panicked. They thought they were surrounded and were running everywhere, making easy targets. I believe you call that a "target enriched environment. It did not take long before the ones left alive were gone. After the dust settled, as they say, we cautiously made contact with the South Vietnamese. They kept asking where the rest of our men were, and we just laughed. We met the Captain (CPT) and I recognized him as the one that had run off and left me to die in the jungle, right after I arrived in country. Instantly, I wanted to kill him, but that would come later. He did not recognize me. We had been out on our mission for about eight days and were not pretty. Nim was moving around through the men and discovered the Captain was a sadistic coward and they hated him. He took twenty percent of their pay every payday, which was a common practice in their army. We stayed with them for the night while they looted the corpses of the fallen.

I could not rest. 'The Fourth Person Within' wanted vengeance. About one in the morning I crept into the Captain's tent and put my hand firmly over his mouth and my face real close to his. I asked him, "Do you remember me, because I surely remember you." A look of panic came over his face as he struggled to get up. "You left me to die, do you remember?" I asked, as I slowly slid the razor-sharp edge of my Bowie knife across his throat. I looked deeply into his eyes and watched as his life slipped slowly away. I had never killed anyone that deliberately before, but he deserved it, and he would not be missed. I crept back to the area with Jack and Nim. Jack took a long look at me with fresh blood covering what was left of my shirt then asked, "Was that the one who left you to die?" "Yes," I said. "Good," he said, and we grabbed a couple of hours rest. In retrospect, it should have bothered me that I could go to sleep right after killing a man like that. Obviously, 'The Fourth Person Within' was in total control. Early morning, we left and headed back to give our report with Nim sporting a fresh stringer of bloody ears hanging from his belt.

We had been at this camp about four and a half months when we started to see a buildup of the enemy soldiers. We knew we would be attacked soon but didn't know when. Finally, our Day of Reckoning came, and we were attacked. The problem we had was that some of our people were turning around in their firing position and firing at us! Knowing that all the guys we recruited were not on our side, Jack and I had quietly planted explosives in every fighting position on the post and had run all the wires back underground to our position during an attack. When someone turned around and pointed his gun in the wrong direction, we selected the right wires, mashed the button, and they disappeared in a big explosion. That put the fear of God in the rest of the enemy soldiers. The battle lasted all day and the A-Team survived with only 4 wounded, - two of which had to be evacuated to a hospital. All 12 were still alive. We lost eighteen Strikers (mercenary soldiers) and there were many, many North Vietnamese troops laying everywhere. God bless the people who invented the 50-caliber machine gun. We piled them up like cord wood and set fire to them. It was a horrible smell. That was the only time our camp got attacked. For the next few months we continued training the Strike Force and running missions for the CIA.

KOREA

My team received orders to go on a special mission in Korea so as soon as replacements arrived, we left. I cannot talk about our mission in Korea, except to say I know what North Korea looked like and we couldn't blend in with the population.

While in Korea, I wanted to improve my language skills so when the rest of the guys went down to the Village to play with the little girls, I was in a Korean Tea house learning proper Korean. I taught the lady what I thought was proper English. She was a nice lady whose family had been deposed from the hierarchy in Seoul, Korea. I went at every opportunity to learn, and when I would leave to go down the street and join my friends she would get upset. I simply told her "Man cannot live by bread alone; he must have a little pork chop every now and then." She said, "You want a girl, I will get you a good girl." About a week later, I went to the tea house and she was all excited, "I got you a girl," she said, "only $400." "Four Hundred Dollars!" I exclaimed that they only cost $2 down the street. Then she brought Cho in, the most beautiful little 16-year-old girl I had ever seen. "Four Hundred Dollars and you own her," she said. "What do you mean, own her?" I asked. She said, "Her father is about to lose the family farm. If you do not buy her, she will be taken to one of the local whorehouses and sold to them." That broke my heart; I could not let that beautiful young girl be sold to a whorehouse, so I bought her. Then I bought a one-room house for $100 dollars for her to live in. That took all the money I could scrape up. I would go down to the village when I could and spend time with her teaching her English. After about two weeks the lady from the tea house stopped me on my way, and asked if there was a problem with Cho, "No!" I said, "We are getting along fine." "But you are not making love to her," she said. "No," I said. "Have you ever looked at us? I am 6 ft. 3 in. tall and weigh about 230 lbs. She is about 5 ft and might weight 100 lbs. at best." "That does not matter" she said, "She thinks because you do not make love to her that you are displeased with her. If you are displeased with her, she has dishonored her family and must kill herself." "You're kidding" I exclaimed, "That is the most ridiculous thing I have ever heard." "Nonetheless, it is the truth," she said. "If you do not make love to her, she will kill herself." What a dilemma, I thought. What am I going to do now? I did the only thing I could do to save her life.

About three weeks later, when I went down to see Cho, she was not there but one of her friends was present. "Where is Cho?" I asked. "She is sick, but do not worry, I am here to take care of you instead." she said. "What do you mean, sick?" I asked, becoming irritated. As it turned out, Cho was having her period and did not want me to have to suffer because of her condition, so she had a friend of hers come over to take her place. I went 'NUTS', and made the young lady take me to get Cho and bring her home where she belonged. I will never understand the thinking of the Oriental mind if I live to be a thousand years old.

Soon after all of this happened, our mission was accomplished, and   it was time to leave. I made sure Cho had enough money to last for about a year. Over there, the daily wage for a 12-hour day was $0.92. I figured with her speaking English now, she could get a job on the post where we had stayed. I often wonder what happen to my cute little Korean lady. I had grown very, very fond of her. Our assignment had been, and probably still is, highly classified.

CUBA

We boarded a plane and headed for San Francisco. This tour over, we had been gone from home well over a year. My mind now was on blond hair and round blue eyes, as we arrived at the San Francisco International Airport. I was headed for Memphis. I heard my name paged over the loudspeaker, "Sergeant Jones report to the American Airlines ticket counter." Knowing there was more than one Sergeant Jones in this world, I ignored the page. There was no way they were looking for me. They paged again, "Sergeant Roy L Jones report to American Airlines ticket counters please." Now they have gotten specific. I could not figure out what they wanted with me.

When I arrived at the ticket counter there were two young military police waiting for me. After asking for my ID which I grudgingly showed them, they told me my orders had been changed. I was to report to Homestead Air Force Base in Florida, and they had my ticket and were supposed to see that I got on the airplane. I laughed and said, "You boys have been watching too much television if you think just you two can make me do anything" as I pushed past them. With that I went over to the bar and ordered a very large drink. It was not long before there were five military police and three Airport police standing around me. There was an older Master Sergeant (MSG) in charge of the group. He sat down and said, "Sarge, I can look at your uniform and all of those patches and that beret and I know not only "who you are, but 'what you are' and we probably do not bother you at all." I looked around laughing and said, "You are right." He said, "Sarge, let's not remodel this part of the airport, we are just trying to do our jobs." We talked for about 30 minutes and I finally said, "Okay I'll go, but

I will not like it."

I landed at Homestead Air Force Base in Florida and finally found out what was up – The Cuban Missile Crisis. We were preparing to invade Cuba, and over the next 6 hours the rest of my team arrived. Our mission was to be dropped in the mountains in the middle of Cuba, disrupt communications and transportation and try to recruit locals to fight Castro.

I was fit to be tied – I had done my duty overseas for well over a year and now. I wanted to go home to Memphis where there were blonde ladies with 'round blue eyes' and a giving spirit. I kept picking up the map and seeing how small Cuba was on the map. I said, "No bigger than that country is we should just go down there and kick everyone's butt and everybody can go home." I did not know until much later how close we had come to a worldwide nuclear war. Finding that out, I broke out in a cold sweat. They only kept us there for about five days and the crisis was over, so off to Memphis I went.

First stop, Rita Watkins house to visit her father and stock up on liquor for the parties I was going to start. My second night in Memphis I found my blonde haired, blue eyed beauty and we spent two glorious days together and I began to settle down. Everyone wanted to know where I had been and what I had been doing and it was like being in the Army. I lied and said, "Nothing to it. you march a lot, and you do exercises. That's pretty much it." I still could not bring myself to tell anyone what I was doing.

My mother was 80 years old before I told her what I had done. She was shocked. I tried to explain to her how I felt about people worrying about me. I just did not want that to be happening. I asked her if she ever thought it was curious that every letter, she wrote me after I got out of basic training was addressed to a post office box in San Francisco. She said she just thought that was the way they did things. My mother would have worried herself sick had she known even ten percent of what I was doing.

I did not realize how much I had changed until one night when a friend of mine and I were driving down the street about 2 a.m. There was a guy beating a girl in the face with his fists in the middle of the road. I shouted "Stop the car! You take care of her; he belongs to me." Just as I got out of the car a squad car pulled up and two police officers got out. My buddy was trying to comfort the girl while I set about killing her boyfriend. Suddenly, she was clawing at my neck and screaming. She was screaming, "Stop, you are going to kill him!" The two police officers pulled me off of him.

The boy and the girl both pressed charges against me for assault and I was arrested. The police officer told me people will do that almost every time. So, the next time, I should just call them and let the police handle it. I informed him the next time, I see such an incident, I will do exactly the same thing. Sitting in jail, I had time to reflect on what had happened and realized if the two police officers had not appeared, I would have killed that boy. This was the first time that 'The Fourth Person Within' had entered the life of the other person that I thought I was, and it scared me really bad. I had to be able to leave that 'Fourth Person Within' in the army and away from my life.

'The Fourth Person Within' is what I call the "Mama Grizzly." This person who can be mean, vicious, and unforgiving. This person shows up when we have seen or experienced more than our mind can process. Sometimes we face two choices: one, roll over and die, or two, stand up and fight back. A lot of people roll over and die. Anyone with a warrior spirit at all will fight back and fight back hard. You will do things you never believed you were capable of doing. Knowing this from personal experience, you become someone you do not like, but you need to survive.

The episode in the middle of the street woke me up. I had to be on guard. That guy abusing that girl pushed every red button in me. I think any male that strikes a female is the lowest form of human life. I cut my leave short and went back to Fort Bragg. NC. While there, one of my buddies was about to go home on his leave and asked me to go with him.

His name was Tarantino and he was from New York City. His father was a retired police officer and originally from Italy. I went with him. Tarantino was what normal people call crazy. For example, we were stopped at a stoplight; the light turned green, the guy behind us immediately hits his horn. Tarantino got out of the car, walked back lifted the guy's hood, reached in and pulled out a handful of wires and threw them in the street. He got back in the car and we went on our merry way. Like I said, normal people call him crazy, but he was one of the best men you could find to back you up in a firefight-gun battle.

One day we wound up in Greenwich Village. Walking down the street a beautiful young lady came out of nowhere and put a necklace around my neck gave me a big hug and a kiss and said, "Wear this always. It will protect you." Then she was gone as fast as she had arrived. It was a small lead mask that was hanging from a leather thong. I still have it. This was the age of the flower children and free love. Tarantino and I wandered Greenwich Village and found the art studio of an artist name Kean. He had become famous for painting sad looking children with great big eyes. I spotted one of his paintings and fell in love with it and bought a print. It is still hanging on my wall; the picture is of a young girl with her arms crossed and the saddest look in those great big eyes that you have ever seen. Every time I look at that picture, I want to hug her and protect her to make her feel safe and secure.

One thing I will say about Italians – they know how to cook, and I love Italian food. Mrs. Tarantino never stopped telling her son and me how skinny we were and that we both needed a wife. You have to love those Italian women. I could only stay for one week until my time was up. It was time to return and become Sergeant Jones again.

We were not back from leave very long before we were sent on a mission to South America. We were to find and neutralize Che Guevara with 'extreme prejudice.' (meaning eliminate him).

Che was Castro's right-hand man. They had gone to school together early in life. When Castro and Che overthrew the Batista government, Che was really the one the people followed. They loved him because he was one of them. When Castro started working with the Soviet Union, Che did not like it; he did not want Cuba to become a Soviet satellite. Castro was afraid of Che because of his influence with the people, so he sent him with a small contingent to Peru to begin to organize people there and to expand Communist influence. He accomplished two things with that one move: he got Che out of his way in Cuba, and he stood to expand his influence into South America.

The United States could not stand idly by and let that happen, therefore, they sent us down there to deal with Che. We were not successful in catching up with him: the closest we got was a warm campfire that had been used the previous night. We estimated his group to be about fifty people. I asked some of my group if anyone thought about 12 guys chasing 50. The only response I got was maybe we should hold back until they pick up some more people. That way it will almost be even. We had spent about two months looking for him when they pulled us out and sent in another team. Now it was time to be sent 'back across the pond', as some say.

VIET NAM – SECOND TRIP

In San Francisco, Jack and I were going to spend our last night in this country partying. We flipped a coin to decide if we would go to a black area or a white area to play. I lost. We arrived at a very large black nightclub about 9:30 and had a couple drinks while we waited for it to fill up.

To be honest, I felt like a grain of salt in a pepper shaker. Now I know what Jack must have felt like all those times he went with me, but he never said a word. There were two cute girls sitting not too far from us and Jack got up and danced with one of them. When he returned, he told me his girl said her friend thought I was cute, so there I went. She said yes, and we were on the dance floor.

It was not long before I began hearing words like 'honky, redneck, and Whitey.' The inevitable happened – someone bumped into me, then challenged me, and took a swing, and all hell broke loose. Out of the corner of my eye I saw people pushed and fly out of the way. It was Jack, coming through the crowd. Now we are standing back-to-back against the world. I will stand back-to-back with Jack Jackson from North Carolina against any number of people anytime. We were doing a lot of damage. After all, we were trained for this.

At long last, a very large police officer named Tiny arrived with several others and put a stop to our fun. Tiny must have weighed 350 pounds easily and carried a ball bat instead of a baton. He spoke with a very loud deep voice and everyone seemed to know and respect him. "What in the devil is going on in here?" he said. The club owner told Tiny that Jack and I had chosen his club in which to spend our last night in this country, and patrons did not like the white guy.

As Tiny swung his bat and hit a man in the mouth, he said, "Is that one of them?" Then he swung at another one. "How about that one?" Now, no one can get hit because they're way too far back. The ambulances began to arrive and haul off bodies. I told Jack we should leave if they would let us. The club owner objected and said we had to stay, and everything was on the house. Tiny said, "If you try to leave, I may have to arrest you," as he laughed and winked. So be it, we stayed and had a great party. We finally slept on the plane.

Our team arrived back in Vietnam and there were a great many more troops in country than there were when we were last there. The team Jack and I were a part of had more personal restrictions than most. The fact that you could not have a tattoo was just one example. The type of missions they sent us on were highly confidential. We dressed in black and did not have dog tags or other personal items. I believe they were looking for deniability. If we were captured or killed, there was nothing to identify us as Americans.

If we were killed, our family would receive a letter that we had died in a parachute accident. We rarely shaved and carried the enemy's weapons, the AK-47. We did not have to worry about resupply of ammunition. If we ran low, we would take it from the bad guys that we had killed. Personally, I carried a very large Bowie knife strapped to my chest upside down, a machete, and a throwing hatchet as well as the AK-47. At that time the AK-47 was far superior to what they gave us, the AR 14. The AR 14 had to be cleaned three times a day and still did not perform. You could bury an AK-47 in the sand under running water and pick it up the next day and it would fire.

We were based out of a camp near the Cambodian border. Over my bunk bed, I put a sign that read, "Ye, though I walk through the valley of the shadow of death, I fear no evil because I am the meanest S.O.B. in this valley." The problem was that I actually believed that.

On one occasion between missions, four of us went to a "Yard Housing-Village" to help the people, by doctoring them as best as we could. We were showing them how to build drainage ditches to carry water and waste away from their houses. We stayed a little longer than we should have. It was almost dark as we were leaving. We heard the enemy soldiers coming into the village from the other direction. We decided to hide and see what happened, I wish we had not done that.

The soldiers were furious that the people had accepted our help and began doing horrific acts on the people. They placed no value whatever on human life or suffering as we know it. One boy had his arm cut off just because he had a bandage on it. Think about the horror of that. They brought all of the villagers to the middle of the village then tied the village chief to a post. Next, they took a steel rod and beat him with it until most of the bones in his body had been broken. That is just one example of what was going on as we watched in horror. They took the chief's ten-year-old daughter and began gang raping her – that was more than my mind could process.

We glanced at each other and as a group rose up and attacked. There were about 40 of them and only four of us, but that did not matter. We had seen more than we could handle, and rage took over. I remember screaming, running and shooting as fast I could. We all did. At some point I lost consciousness. There was about fifteen minutes of time that I do not remember. When I came back mentally, I was standing there with my Bowie knife in one hand, my machete in the other, my gun on the ground, and bodies and parts of bodies lying everywhere. I was covered in gore.

Evidently, we had run out of ammunition. The Viet Cong were either all dead or gone. More of the villagers were dead and wounded having been caught in the crossfire. All four of us were still alive although two of my buddies had been wounded. Neither one of them had bad wounds. All of us were bleeding from cuts all over our bodies. We had to take a little time to evaluate our situation. The young boy whose arm had been cut off had bled to death. It was now dark with the exception of the cooking fires. We did what we could to patch up the villagers, and ourselves before leaving for our camp. About a mile from the village was a clear mountain stream. I laid down face up and let the water run over me trying to remove some of the gore from my body. But no amount of water could wash out my mind that fifteen-year-old boy who had joined the National Guard. He was long since gone and he had been taken over by 'The Fourth Person Within.'

What happened in that village was not that unusual for the enemy. That was the way they operated, "with terror." If the villagers did not cooperate 100% with them, unspeakable things were done to them. They also took all the young men with them along with all the food they wanted. The villagers were left with almost nothing on which to survive. If you have any compassion at all, you wanted to help these people. It soon had become evident that the only way to help them was to treat the opposition forces the way they treated the villagers. So, we did.

The Viet Cong were masters of booby traps, so I developed my skill with booby traps. I soon learned the art of misdirection for example, after I set a tripwire. I would go down the trail about 10 yards and break a small limb on a tree or a bush or place a small piece of cloth hanging from a limb, just to create something that was out of place. The target would then be concentrating on what was out of place and not pay close attention to where he stepped. Bye bye, bad guy.

My favorite weapon was the Claymore Mine. The Claymore was a small piece of C-4 explosive that contained, if my memory serves me correctly, a fourth of a mile of steel wire crimped every fourth of an inch thus creating thousands of tiny pieces of steel and a devastating blast. A favorite of the opposition force soldiers was to dig a hole in the ground then put sharpened punji sticks in the bottom then cover it up. They dipped the sharp end of the sticks in dung thus assuring instant infection.

The punji stick was not designed to kill but to wound. We learned that if you would put punji sticks in the grass along the trail out of sight when a patrol would come down the trail at the right time you shoot the first two guys and the rest of them dive off the trail right on top of the punji sticks. Learning from them, we began collecting the heads of poisonous snakes. We would milk poison out and put it on the tips of our bullets so if the target was only wounded, they would still die.

On this tour we had access to helicopters. When we were sent into enemy territory on a mission to bring back prisoners for interrogation, we also devised a plan that required timing, but worked like a charm. Since this system worked best at night, we had a night scope for our sniper rifle from a British catalog. The United States did not at that time have a night scope.

We would set Claymore mines strategically along the trail pointing them slightly upwards, so they destroyed anything 2 feet above the ground and up. We would shoot the third guy back in line in the leg and push the button on the Claymore at the same time the guy would go down. As the Claymore mines went off everyone would die but him. Usually the third guy back was the one in charge. We would then grab him, throw him over our shoulder and run like the devil for the extraction point. Now every human being within 5 miles knows we're there and it is not a safe place to be. We did this on a number of occasions and pulled it off all but one time. There were more opposition force soldiers in the area than we had expected. Thus, when we got to the extraction point, we were surrounded and were fighting for our lives. I knew I was going to die right there!

Helicopter pilots were a crazy bunch who had no fear. I will be honest with you, I do not know if I would have flown in there to get us if I were them, but they came anyway. They flew right into a hail of bullets, and we ran like the devil for the helicopter. I was carrying our prisoner and threw him in the door so hard he almost came out the other side. The door-gunner had to grab him as he slid through. We got away. This is one of those times in my life that God was holding his protective hand over me.

When we landed back at the base, I hugged the pilots and the door gunners like I was a little girl. I told the pilots how crazy I thought they were for coming in to get us. They just laughed and said we were just talking about how crazy you guys are for having been there in the first place. The helicopter was riddled with bullet holes, but none had hit a vital spot. Thank you, God. That day, I promised myself that one day I would own a helicopter.

I have no idea how many VC Jack, Nim, and I were responsible for killing or how many innocent people got hurt or died in our booby traps. I do know that for some reason I felt no remorse and that bothered me. All I am really sure of is that we amassed a very large body count. I also came to know we three had a bad reputation among the enemy for our effectiveness.

We were given a mission to neutralize a double agent. They never tell you directly to kill someone. They say things like, "We need to deal with this individual with extreme prejudice because he speaks out of both sides of his mouth." We met this little guy on the outskirts of a small village on the Laotian border like we had six or seven times before and exchanged packages. Nim did the deed and we collected our packages and disappeared into the night leaving no sign that we had been there with the exception of the dead man. Mission accomplished.

Unfortunately, because 'The Fourth Person Within' was in total control it did not emotionally bother me. To Jack, Nim, and me, it was little more than swatting a fly. In my saner moments, this is what I hated the most. Life and death meant very little, just like the bad guys, we were dealing with. I guess we were no better than they were. We were fighting terror with terror and that is the only way you could really win. but at what price?

When Jack, Nim, and I went on missions, we performed as if

we were one person. Talking was not necessary. Body language was all that was necessary. We knew each other so well that our movements spoke volumes. We were a finely tuned team. Our missions varied a lot; exchanging packages, bringing back prisoners to interrogate, assassinating a village chief or one of a dozen other crazy things military command wanted done. We were officially called advisers, but we did very little advising. We mostly did covert operations that left no tracks back to the U.S. Army.

TIGER PAWS

Coming back from a patrol, Jack, Nim, and I found some very large tiger foot prints in the mud by a stream. Jack said we had something similar to plaster of Paris back at camp, so we retrieved it and made tiger foot print molds. We did not share what we had done with anyone else.

Sometimes, we would be checking the guards in the early hours of the morning, and find them dozing off and not alert to guard the perimeter. Our strikers did not put the same emphasis on staying awake while on guard duty as we did. About two weeks after we made the molds, Jack and I were checking the perimeter about three-thirty in the morning and found the guards asleep. We made tiger tracks in front of one of the firing positions as if the tiger had been looking at the guards while they slept. We fired up into the air and screamed TIGER, TIGER. Everyone went crazy, and began shooting and screaming. The funny thing was everyone saw the tiger running away and shot at him. When the guards saw how close the tiger had been, it had a profound effect and to the best of my knowledge, we did not have anymore problems with the guards dozing off on perimeter duty.

In our quiet time, Jack and I talked a lot about the changes we saw in each other, and we did not like the changes. The fact that we were still alive gave mute testimony to the fact that for this period of time the changes might have been necessary for us to survive. Jack and I were a part of a 12-man team that operated in small groups. I loved it that way. Four people or less can disappear a lot easier than a larger group. Becoming a part of the landscape is easier if you knew what you're doing, and we did.

For a while, I seemed to get worse every day. We would go out of our way to hurt the enemy. I hate to say it, but I detested them, and I wanted them all dead. I had learned the difference between fear and terror. You cannot fight terror with fear. You lose every time. If every time I see you, I hit you in the mouth with my fist, you will be afraid of me. That is called fear. If every time I see you, I cut one of your fingers or toes off, you will be terrified of me. That is called terror.

We were responding to them with terror, and the opposition soldiers were terrified of us. I saw a wanted poster with my name on it one day. If you brought in the head of Sergeant Jones, you would be rewarded with three year's pay. Jack had one also. That is a lot of money. I wish I had kept one to remind me of what I do not ever want to become again.

To deal with 'The Fourth Person Within' you have to first understand where he came from and why he is there. You can never forget all the things that you did or all the things that you witnessed. You and God together have to deal with those situations. Without His help, I would never have survived. Some people try to drown 'The Fourth Person Within' with alcohol. Some try to hide him with drugs. Some even commit suicide to try to escape 'The Fourth Person Within!'

Some of us recognize him for what he is. I believe 'The Fourth Person Within' is actually trying to help us keep our sanity. That may sound like a contradiction, but it really is not. When you experience events that you cannot mentally process you have a place for your mind to go. That is why 'The Fourth Person Within' is there, to help us survive until we can get to a better place. Jack and I talked about this a lot. I do not know what I would have done without Jack Jackson being my friend. Evidently the changes that had taken place within us were obvious to everyone else because Jack and I drew fewer and fewer missions. This gave us the time to begin to deal with 'The Fourth Person Within.'

GOING HOME

Our tour was up, and it was time to go back to the other world. We began trying to prepare ourselves for this. At the airfield, I walked over to the edge of the jungle and sat down. I began to talk to 'The Fourth Person Within' like there was a real person sitting there. I told him he had to stay here, because he did not belong where I was going. "You do not fit in I said, talking out loud. As I sat there talking to that person, I felt his presence after about ten or fifteen minutes. I got up and walked back to the plane. As I walked up the ramp to the plane, I looked back to where I had been sitting and could almost swear I saw him sitting there with his hand in the air, as if to say, "I will be here if you need me."

Jack and I had a quiet trip back toward the world, each of us dealing with our inner selves in his own way. Of one thing we were sure; that we never wanted to experience what we had gone through again. We arrived at Schofield Barracks in Hawaii about 11 p.m., or 2300 hours, as the Army would say, and we were starving to death. We just knew it was going to be 5:30 in the morning before we would be able to eat.

An Airman walked up and said, "If you guys are hungry, the mess hall is right over there," and pointed to a large building. We were shocked. "You mean its open now," I asked, "Oh yes," he said. "They're open 24 hours a day." We walked into this "Palace of a mess hall." I walked up to the line, and a cook said, "What can I get you sir?" I laughed and said, "A big old steak would do just fine." "How would you like that cooked sir," he asked, and I almost dropped my teeth. "You mean I can have one?" I asked. He said, "I have some steaks back here and you're welcome to anything we have."

Jack and I enjoyed the best meal we had eaten in well over a year and decided that we should have joined the Air Force. I had no idea that anyone in the service lived like those guys. I had a newfound respect for the Air Force guys; they seemed to know what we had been through and tried in every way to show their appreciation. It was great.

We arrived back in the States and immediately got tattoos on our left arms that read "Born to Raise Hell," My enlistment was about up, so Jack and I went our separate ways. I am sad to say that was the last time I saw him. "Jack Jackson from North Carolina, wherever you are, may God bless you for being there for me when I needed you the most. You are the best friend a person could ever have. Thank you so much."

Now, my main goal in life was to guard against the return of 'The Fourth Person Within.' A lot of men, over the years, have gone off to war and have had similar experiences. Soldiers are never the same because we are all different people, but they are still similar. Some of them have figured out and were able to walk away from the 'The Fourth Person Within.' They have to keep their guard up or he will return. Never push an old veteran around. He will not dance with you and box in the parking lot. He will, however, kill you in a sudden and most violent way.

My enlistment was about up, and it had been five long years since I had gotten on that bus with 43 strangers to go to Fort Leonard Wood Missouri. I had lived a very different kind of life than I could have ever expected. In some small ways, I was a 23-year-old young man and in some ways, I felt like I was 100 years old and all but worn out. My values of life and death had changed, so I needed to work on that part of myself. In some ways, I was a walking time bomb and had to be very careful working to fit in with what we will call "normal people." I spent my leave by myself trying to decide what I wanted to do next. I decided, I enjoyed army life for the most part, but I did not want to do the job I had been doing. I decided that if I was going to stay in the army, I should probably become a General. For that to happen I had to go to Officer Candidate School. So, I took all the tests necessary and blew right through them. On the IQ test, all you had to score was 125, and my score was 148.

I received my orders to go to Officer Candidate School (OCS) in Oklahoma, but there were several months before class would begin. In the meantime, orders sent me to Fort Campbell Kentucky to do odd jobs. I taught classes in hand-to-hand combat for the Recondo School. That was fun. On occasions, HQ orders sent me across country to pick up prisoners. On one such excursion they sent me and another sergeant to California to pick up a prisoner and bring him back. When they turned him over to us, he laughed and said, "They sent a Green Beret with a gun to pick me up? They must think I am some sort of desperate character." He then looked at me and said, "You wouldn't shoot me if I took off, would you?" I said, "Why don't you take off and we'll both find out." I don't think he liked the look on my face, so he shut up. I told him that I was a crack shot and I would not shoot him to kill him, but he would never have sex again and he would walk funny the rest of his life.

It was November 1963. Over the loudspeaker on the train it was announced that our president, John F. Kennedy, had been shot in Texas. Our prisoner thought that was humorous. "I did not like him anyway," he said. Now I don't know if you have ever seen the bathroom compartment on a train, but they are tiny. I made this guy drop his pants, sit on the commode, and then I handcuffed his hands behind the commode in a very uncomfortable position. I left him there for 10 or 12 hours.

When I finally let him go, he started talking about turning me in for torturing him. I told him what a shame it would be if he tried to escape and fell off the train at 80 miles an hour out in the middle of nowhere still handcuffed. He shut up. When we arrived back at Fort Campbell, I was summoned to the office. This very large Master Sergeant (MSG) told me I was about to be sent back across the pond with my old team. I corrected him and said, "No, I have Orders to go to Officer Candidate School and that is my intention."

He told me, "I took care of all of that. You don't need to be an officer. You need to get it straight in your head boy, that you are a lifer and for the rest of your life you are going to do what people just like me tell you to, and I will never have to salute you." At that moment I mentally got out of the US Army and told him under those circumstances I would not reenlist, and they could not send me anywhere with just a couple of months left on my enlistment.

FINISHED WITH U.S. ARMY FOREVER

I quietly served my remaining time and was discharged. They gave me a copy of my military records and when I looked at them, I did not know who this person was. That Master Sergeant eliminated everything I had done since basic training and replaced it with a person I did not know. In those days, all records were done with pen, pencil, and typewriter in triplicate. It was not a big deal to lose a few pages and replace them with new pages. That Master Sergeant effectively eliminated me as a human being and replaced me with another one.

I felt like I had been used and discharged. They had no idea the effect all that had on me. That is why I have not had any contact with the U.S. Army since. I only recently openly admitted to being a Veteran. I am proud of what I did for my country and would live through it again, if necessary.

I left Fort Campbell and the United States Army forever. I had no plans or idea what I was to do with myself; or what I should do. But I decided that when I pulled out of Gate 4 at Fort Campbell, I would let the flow of traffic decide for me which direction to go. I could have landed in Louisville, Kentucky, Knoxville, Tennessee, Birmingham, Alabama, or Memphis, but it did not matter to me. The flow of traffic took me toward Memphis. When I got home and surprised my mother, I took everything I had from the United States Army except my beret, put it in a pile in the backyard, soaked it in gasoline and set fire to it. I wanted nothing more to do with the Army.

The first job I got was with Dover Elevator Corporation at Bullfrog Corners, Mississippi – just over the state line. I made $1.60 an hour to unload trucks. On the wall there was a billboard where they listed all the available jobs in the plant and since every job paid more than mine, I signed up for every one of them. After a while I was accepted as a timer maker. The timer opens and closes the doors and makes the elevator go up and down. The foreman took me to this little room and showed me all of the transistors and such that I would need. He gave me a schematic and a desk with a soldering iron and lamp on it. He said make these until you have made 400 of them and he left.

How he knew that I knew how to read a schematic is a mystery to me. I assembled all the parts I needed and went to work. After a short period of time I was organized and producing four timers an hour feeling pretty good about myself. Foreman Guy stopped by my workstation and told me that I could not make four timers an hour. I said, "Yes, I can, and I think I can get to five if I keep working at it." He said, "You do not understand. The book says all you have to make is three in an hour, and if you are doing four, the rest of us will be expected to do four." I said, "Then you guys need to get the lead out," and kept working.

I was not there to make friends. I was there to do a job and get paid for it. When I got my second check, I noticed a $5 deduction I had not seen before. I went to the office to ask what the deduction was and was told that it was union dues. "Union dues?" I asked, "I did not join any union." He said, "But this is a union plant, all three hundred and four employees belong to the union." I replied, "But, I don't want to join the union, and I want my $5 back." That started a heck of a mess. I went back to my bench - mad as I could be. Word spread throughout the plant that I was anti-union and everyone's attitude toward me changed. No one seemed to like me anymore.

The next day, as I was walking through the gravel parking lot to get to my car, four guys decided they were going to show me the error of my ways. I spotted a small pile of two-by-fours over by the fence and got to them before they did." I wore those guys out with a two-by-four. I had to chase the fourth one, but I caught him. Then I calmly walked over to my car and went home. The next day, I went to work just to prove that they had not run me off, but when I left that day, it was for good.

My uncle, Gene Gardner, was an electrician and was working on a parking garage for Sears at Crosstown. Sears wanted that garage finished before Thanksgiving, so they were working three shifts a day, seven days a week. I went out there with my uncle one morning and got a job as a laborer making $2.10 an hour. It was a union job, and although I have nothing against unions, that's something that should be discussed when you're hired. You could work as many hours as you wanted to, so I signed up two eight hour shifts a day, 4 days a week and one 8-hour shift on Friday, Saturday, and Sunday. I believe that is 88 hours a week. All over 40 hours was overtime.

I knew I had to keep myself busy and besides that, I was making a fortune. After two or three weeks, I took a job on Friday and Saturday night as a bouncer in a nightclub called "The Cipango Club" at 4th and Court downtown. The guy said, "You can have all you want to drink, all the ladies you can handle, and I will give you $20 a night." I asked him, "If I'm going to get all of that, what do I want with $20?" He said, "You may want to get a motel room." I said, "Okay, I'll take the money."

That was one of the most enjoyable jobs I've ever had. There were five bouncers and I was the second smallest. The sailors and the "Rednecks" would fight every Friday and Saturday night. We had a ball. When a pretty girl would come in by herself I felt it was my duty to join her because if I didn't, there would be no question that "Rednecks" and sailors would fight over her. Just doing my job, you see. That lasted about three months, but all those hours and very little sleep is what I needed – I had to stay busy.

We finished the parking garage and then I had very little to do. Most of my checks had not been cashed and were stacked on a dresser at home. One day I read an ad in the Memphis paper, "Be one of New York City's finest – Riot Control at $166 a week to start – 6 foot, 190 lb. minimum to apply." Sounded like fun so I called them, because I had had riot control training in the service. They hired me over the telephone.

I called the Tarantino family that I had met while on leave with my buddy. They were excited that I was coming and offered me their son's apartment in their basement. These were truly nice people. When I arrived, Mr. Tarantino took me to the local hardware store and told me to pick out a hatchet handle. I did. It was put in a brown paper bag with the receipt stapled at the top. Mr. Tarantino told me to carry it with me everywhere I went until I was issued a gun. It was not a safe place there since riots were going on all over town.

Mrs. Tarantino told me I was one of the few people she had ever met who had manners, but I had two problems: number one, I was skinny and needed to eat more. number two, I was single. I should find a nice girl and get married – after all, I was 24 years old. Mrs. Tarantino set about trying to solve both of my perceived problems. Every night when I came home there was a pot of something being kept warm on the small stove in my apartment. Most of the time I did not know what it was, but it always tasted great and I ate it all.

I soon learned that the ladies up North really liked my accent. I would enter a local bar and order a beer and before I could drink it the bartender would bring me another one and say "This is from those ladies over there at that table. They want to know if you will join them." So, I did. Also, I loved that... the slower I talked, the more they liked my Southern accent.

Needing to stay busy, I got a part-time job at JCPenney as a Store Detective. There was a bank in the subway system below JCPenney but it was not open on Saturday. One of the managers asked me if I would go down the street about four blocks to another bank and buy $500 worth of dimes. Off I went on my little errand, and on my way back a wino stepped in front of me with a straight razor and said, "Give me the money." Five Hundred dollars worth of dimes is quite heavy, so I said, "Here you go," and I put it on his shoulder as he backed away. He kept threatening me with that straight razor. When he got about 6 feet away, I pulled my gun, and had him drop the razor. After which, I had him walk in front of me and carry the dimes.

When we got back to the store, I gave the dimes to the manager and asked him to call an ambulance and the police. I took the wino into the security room and discussed him threatening me with that straight razor. By that time, he could not stand up any longer. The ambulance came and took him to the hospital. After that night in Night Court, the judge let him go. I was glad he and I had our discussion privately.

In 1964, there were a lot of riots in New York City. After a refresher course, and I was assigned to a unit. On our first assignment, I faintly heard a girl scream as we passed the ally. I left the squad and ran down the alley. There were two guys trying to rape a young girl. I quickly broke up that little game and the two guys took off running. I shouted, "Stop or I'll shoot!" They did not stop, so I shot them both right in the buttocks. I made sure that the girl was okay, then went to check on the two guys. I wanted them both to remember what you do not do to ladies. As a matter of fact, I wanted them to have a problem every time they even thought about ladies, and where I shot them, I believe I accomplished my assignment. The shots brought out all kinds of people. The girl was shaking from the incident, but she was going to be okay since I had arrived just in time.

For shooting those guys, I got into all kinds of trouble, it seems as though the rule was if no one's life was in immediate danger, you do not shoot. They asked me why I shot them, "Why did you not chase them?" they asked. I answered by saying "You issued me a pistol, not running shoes." I was becoming irritated with their attitude and they thought I was a smart aleck. They took my pistol and gave me another baton, which made me very unhappy.

Shortly afterwards, we were involved in a downtown riot. We were moving the crowd in front of us up the street, when I saw a man come into a second-floor window with a pistol. It looked like it was pointed at me. All I could do was scream, "He has a gun!" and throw one of those stupid sticks at him. He shot a man standing next to me in the throat, killing him instantly. I went nuts. And I charged into the crowd - headed for that building. I had not made it more than ten feet and the crowd had me down stomping and kicking me.

My guys pushed forward and rescued me. The medics patched me up and they sent me home for the rest of the night. As soon as I got home, after putting my belongings in my car, I pointed my car south. I drove all night and until the next morning. I pulled off the highway at an overlook and watched the sun come up. I was in Virginia and the sunrise and the mountains were beautiful. Sitting there for a long time, I talked to God and promised him that if He would just let me get back to Tennessee, He would never have to worry about me going back to New York again.

The next day, I made it back to Tennessee. Now I had to figure out what I was going to do with my life. I did not want to be a soldier, and I didn't want to be a Police Officer. This is the point where my first book titled "<u>Life and Times of a Serial Restaurateur</u>" begins.

In 1995, at a church on Old Hickory Boulevard in Nashville Tennessee, God reached down and touched me. I was on my knees and begging for His forgiveness for all the bad things that I had done in my life. The pastor of that church Brother Jack Batson was praying for me as well as were most of the people in the church. At some point I felt the words... "My Son You Are Forgiven" ... the greatest moment in my life. At that, my life changed. I was now clean as the driven snow. All my sins and shortcomings were forgiven. The demons from my past that were always with me seemed to go away. At that point I could talk openly about what I had done. I now knew I no longer needed 'The Fourth Person Within.'

THE FOURTH PERSON WITHIN

Honors

1. Honorary Governor State of Ohio
2. Awarded the Rank of Lieutenant Colonel (LTC) – as Aide-de-Camp to the Governor's Staff in Georgia (Personal assistant and Secretary)
3. Kentucky Colonel – The highest title of honor bestowed by the Commonwealth of Kentucky.
4. Tennessee Squire – position of honor from the Jack Danial's Distillery – the top selling American Whiskey in the world.
5. Honorary Sheriff – Davidson County, Tennessee
6. Graduate of Wharton School of Managers and Acquisitions
7. Graduate of Dale Carnegie Course
8. Asked to be KING for Marti Gras "Bards of Bohemia" in New Orleans, Louisiana

When I took all of this list of awards to a Kroger store for recognition, I was told, "That is very nice, but would you step over to the side. The person behind you has cash."

ABOUT THE AUTHOR—ROY JONES

I have lived a wonderful, many faceted life. God has blessed me a lot more than I could ever deserve. I live in the great metropolis of Trenton, Tennessee, a town of about 4,000 people. My son is the Pastor of the First United Methodist Church in Trenton, where I am a member. My other son is a computer expert in Omaha, Nebraska, and my daughter is an aesthetician living in Nashville, Tennessee. The people here are the greatest people in the world, and accept me for what I am. I do some consultant work in the restaurant business, after 53 years in the industry. My first book was *The Life and Times of a Serial Restaurateur* - AMAZON. I have helped with a prison ministry and taught classes in the jail for incarcerated men. Presently, I am helping my son by cooking for a food catering mission for people in need- **WHY NOT MINISTRIES**. I sometimes am asked to speak to groups of people on a variety of subjects. Somewhere there is a reason that God has held his protective hand over me for so long.

E-mail Roy Jones (brotherroyjones@gmail.com)

Made in the USA
Columbia, SC
05 October 2024

43105050R00055